The Epic of Timothy Gray

By A.W. Clark

This edition published by NXiL MEDiA
www.nxilmedia.com

ISBN 979-8-9957354-0-3

The following story is completely true, as far as I know, and takes place in south central Oklahoma in the spring of 1971.

Chapter One
A Chance Meeting

In a wide open meadow, under a full moon and clear sky blanketed with stars, lies a small mouse, sprawled out in the muddy bank of a creek. Fur mangled and stained with blood, his red cape spread out like a blanket drew every eye of the meadow with great concern. It is the hunting hour. No tiny creature is safe, especially not one so exposed to the forest tree line with no cover or shelter. All the critters of the creek seemed to shriek out with heartbreak. The songs of insects drowning out the low flow of creek water. Suddenly a dead silence falls on the entire meadow. One can almost hear the faint whimper of the mouse. Everyone knows what is about to happen, but fear paralyzes the entire spectrum of life on the meadow as a winged shadow glides out from the forest trees. A collective breath is held as every other tiny critter of the meadow is conflicted with heartbreak and gratitude that they are not the target of the owls' evening hunt. From the tall reeds a voice shouts through the silence, "look out!" The owl slows his ascent for a brief moment to ensure it is safe but then seizes the opportunity and with targeted focus dives down toward his prey.

The mouse takes a deep breath. The next few moments take place very quickly. To the outside observer, it was over in a flash. A mist of blood and feathers, flapping and twitching. A fight unlike any in the meadow had ever seen. One might not have questioned an injured creature who had just given up on life, but this was in no way the case. Upon closer inspection one might have noticed that the mouse did not close his eyes in fear, but instead was looking head on into the approaching threat with a sense of anticipation. One might even begin to question if his whimpering was sadness or antagonism. Most cringe and turn their eyes at the climax of a violent moment, but if one had looked closely, they would have learned that things are not always as they seem.

As the owl extended its talons, spreading them wide, the mouse rolled to its side to reveal a long sharpened stick hidden under his cape. The long stick covered in dirt, once lifted up, extended well beyond the mouse's position and appeared to be hinged under a rock. The owl had no time to react and knowing nothing but the thirst of flesh it had no inclination of breaking off its attack. As the owl reached its target, the mouse thrust the spear into the air impaling the owl directly below the neck. The mouse now lay in the clutches of the owl's talons, but the owl's flight was halted and its injuries fatal. Not even the owl had fully understood what had taken place, attempting to fly, unaware of the grounding rod through its collar. The fury of flapping movements that followed were difficult to watch. Still wrapped in the owl's talons, the mouse drew a razor sharp blade from his belt and sliced through the tendon above the talon. Instantly he was flung from the owl's grasp and into the creek bed.

The owl now lay still, panting and wheezing. It was losing control of its extremities as it still twitched and squirmed. The owl was in shock. For as long as it could remember, no tiny creature from the meadow had ever been anything more than a tear soaked meal. None had ever so cruelly fought against the natural order of life. "How?", the owl whispered. "How is this possible?" The figure of the mouse emerged from the creek, dripping wet and in its hand, the razor, but in its eyes a fiery rage. "You feed on the sorrow of families. You target the weak and the small. Your judgment has arrived." The mouse walked up onto the owl and was now standing on his chest looking down on him, one hand holding the end of the stick now penetrating and pinning the bird to the ground and his other hand wielding his blade, a small curved piece of surgical steel. "Who do you think you are?", the owl spat out, disgusted to have his meal standing on him. "Shhhh" the mouse said as he pressed down on the stick causing the owl to shutter in pain. "Unlike your victims you swallow whole, this will be over far too soon." With that, the mouse slid the knife slowly across the neck of the owl with a smooth but forceful motion. Blood drained into the creek bed forming small rivers that fed into the stream. The mouse stood there with hate in his eyes as he watched life fade from the eyes of the confused bird of prey. When he was satisfied that the moment had passed, he began cleaning his blade with some feathers he had plucked from the underside of the massive bird.

As he sheathed his sword and took a deep breath, he began to weep, leant against the carcass of the owl. His mournful cry grew deeper until he was disturbed by rustling in the nearby tall grass. He froze for a moment and slowly placed his hand on the tang of his blade. "Speak up, the last beast who tried to sneak up on me just surrendered his life to my blade!" the mouse shouted out into the wall of grass. He wiped the tears from his eyes and sat up. Squinting his eyes, he could see a large figure emerging from the tall grass.

Slowly and carefully stepping through the brush, about three times the size of the mouse, was an opossum with dark ears and a pale white face. "I seek no trouble, no trouble at all" the opossum spoke, timidly lowering his head and sniffing the ground. The mouse looked the opossum up and down and then turned his back to him and began plucking feathers from the owl carcass. "I suppose that it was you who cried out a warning to my trap?"

"I am sorry, I intended to warn you." The opossum explained as it approached from the tall reeds. "I apologize for my misplaced assumption of danger." He said with confused amazement. "I thought the owl was hunting you, but now I see it was the other way around."

"That is a mighty fine trophy you have there" the opossum said, slowly waddling closer and looking longingly at the animal flesh. "I have never seen a small creature fight with such veracity" the opossum said inquisitively, "You are not from this meadow are you?"

As he began bundling stacks of feathers together the mouse, somewhat distracted, responded, "NO. Well, yes but no. I was born nearby, just up stream below the great oak tree, but I have been gone for a while."

"I thought you looked familiar" the opossum declared, "you are one of the Gray litter!"

The mouse froze as if he had seen a fright. "Yes, my mother was Evelyn Gray" the mouse said softly, "Did you know of her?"

"Oh yes. Dreadful thing what happened to your mother, she was a fine lady. The rumor in the breeze was that none of the gray litter survived." The opossum spoke delicately as if hiding a question in his statement, and then after an awkward pause inquired, "I don't suppose you would mind if I helped you with this."

The opossum stuck his nose directly into the neck wound of the owl and began gnawing upon the flesh.

The mouse twisted his face with distaste and responded.

The Epic Of Timothy Gray

"Sure, help yourself. And you can call me Timothy."

The opossum brought his head up to meet Timothy. His face now stained red with blood just below his eyes. He licked his lips and spoke, "Very nice to meet you Timothy. I am Tobias Greenbottom, but you may call me Toby."

He looked back down to the now gnawed opening of the bird carcass with a large smile. "I have never had the pleasure of a warm meal such as this!" He crawled back down and began to grind his teeth through bone and flesh.

Timothy climbed down from the piled remains of the owl and began gathering his things. He stitched together the large delicate feathers into four tightly bundled packs, all connected with string that Timothy was tying around his waist.

As he fastened his last knot and adjusted his blade tucked into his belt, he paused for a moment and looked back at the curled tail of the opossum's backside. He opened his mouth to speak, but then contemplated. He looked up into the stars and then turned toward the bank of the stream and set off, disappearing into the thick blades of grass dragging the feathers behind.

Toby instantly popped his head out from the bird to see the feathers disappearing into the thick. Blood now dripped from his chin, his dark pointy eyes slowly panned from side to side. The sounds of the forest had returned and seemed to be amplified in that moment. The breeze through the pale green brush and the howling wind above caused his hair to stand up on the back of his neck. Toby stepped away, moving slowly, attempting to act subtle, but then gradually increasing in speed as his heart began racing with fear.

As Toby came to a clearing he quickly slowed down to not expose himself to his surroundings. There, at the rocks by the creek, was Timothy. He was gathering and laying feathers out onto the ground while weaving them together into a pattern. Timothy had noticed the bright red nose, still stained with blood, poking out of the tall reeds. Timothy called out in a soft but confident voice, "Did you abandon your feast so soon?"

Toby slowly emerged from the grass.

"I find it best to not linger around a fresh kill site at this time of night... the smells tend to attract competition."

Toby spoke softly as he ventured to the stream edge to have a drink. Pausing every few steps to look in a frozen stance to observe his surroundings, all while Timothy continued diligently, hopping around his strange crafted object, pulling feathers from one end through to the other.

Timothy showed no sign of concern for the opossum, or anything in his surroundings. He seemed to have a crazed dedication to the task at hand. Toby's attention was drawn to Timothy and his efforts. There was nothing normal about this to Toby. He kept his eyes on Timothy as he drank from the creek.

"Do you find it wise to build your nest out in the open?" Toby asked, trying not to seem rude. Timothy paused for a moment and looked down at what he was building. "I suppose this does look like a fine nest I am making" He continued to sculpt upwards on what was beginning to look exactly like a bird's nest made of feathers and grasses.

"So it is not a nest then sir?" Toby asked while walking closer to inspect.

"No, my whiskered friend, a nest it is not" Timothy looked up, proudly smiling as he had just put in the final feather. He then glanced over into the tall reeds and bolted towards them.

Toby's eyes got wide as he looked upon the bowl shaped basket made of feathers.

Timothy began gnawing at a large dried reed plant until he had knocked it down to the ground. Toby watched with excitement and curiosity. This level of action and activity was highly unusual at this time of night. It was somewhat comforting to Toby to be so close to such an active creature in the open. Surely if they are spotted by a predator, this mouse jumping about will be the target of an attack and not himself, Toby thought as Timothy chewed on the reed, flattening it out on one end.

Timothy took the long reed into his mouth and began flipping his feathered creation end to end until it flopped over, slowly getting closer to the stream.

Timothy turned and spoke to the opossum who was clearly still confused, so much now that his head was beginning to tilt to the side.

"It has been a pleasure to become acquainted with you Toby, but I am afraid, where I now go, you will not be able to follow." He turned his head down to the ground. "This journey is for me alone", his eyes reconnected now, "Seek safe shelter. Goodbye friend. I wish you a long life and many warm meals to come."

With that, Timothy flipped his not-a-nest again one last time and it flopped into the creek. He placed the reed back into his mouth and then jumped into the bowl shaped nest afloat in the water. He used the reed to push off from the rocks and into the current of the stream. Quickly he faded into the slowly rising fog over the creek and was swept into the current and out into wide rushing water.

Toby walked out to the water's edge and then down into his reflection in the moonlight. No one had ever called him "friend" before, he thought, as a smile came over his face. Suddenly, he became aware again of every sound coming from the nearby forest. The hoot of a distant owl sent shivers down his spine. He slowly backed away from the stream and then quickly scurried into the safety of the tall grasses.

Chapter Two
Feathers Float

The fog was rising from the steaming waters. Timothy navigated the rough twists of current until the water calmed, as it opened wide into a much larger river. The waters went almost still as the surface became a smooth mirror, reflecting the stars and the cowering trees from the nearby forest. The night was still and silent, but the trees of the forest seemed to have many eyes looking down upon this oddity of a mouse, floating out into open waters on a boat made of feathers. Timothy's reed no longer touched the bottom. The water was deep and he dared not look too deeply into it. Timothy was exhausted and in a rare moment of quiet, laid down in his boat looking up into the clear night sky. It had been a while since he had just taken a moment to sit still and rest. Seeing as there was nothing he could do to expedite his journey across the river, he found it best to just be still and not attract any attention.

The Epic Of Timothy Gray

Timothy gazed into the stars, always checking his bearings with the north star, remembering fondly how his mother had taught him to navigate the night to find his way home. He came from a long line of skilled scavengers, for Timothy was a field mouse. Every winter was a right of passage; the young field mice would venture into the nearby buildings that sprawled the hillside of the prairie. It was always the north star that would guide him back to the mighty oak in the spring. It was on his last trip home that everything changed. That mighty oak that once represented family and the comforts of home would now be seen as a tombstone in Timothy's eyes. Ironically, it was on that day of returning home that he learned how feathers float upon the water. Haunting memories seem to lash out at him. Memories can be conflicting to the soul. For how can you remember the face of your mother, but not suddenly recall the violent end to her life carried out in front of you. Timothy curled into a ball floating adrift in his own past, forcing himself to recall if only for the opportunity to see her face again.

It had been an interesting winter for Timothy. He had ventured farther than any of his family. Against the wisdom and wishes of his mother, he had gone to spend winter in a hunting lodge that was sometimes inhabited by humans. For as much as Timothy had been taught to avoid humans, he also found them supremely fascinating. It was that winter that Timothy first discovered what is referred to as human magic. In the lodge, he had encountered a pack rat by the name of Philip that introduced Timothy in the art of written word. Philip had accumulated many scraps of paper and even a few full length novels in the sub-flooring of the hunting shack. Timothy had taken such an interest in reading that he didn't return home on the first warm night of spring but instead chose to finish reading a tale penned by the author Alexandre Dumas, in which he had become so absorbed that he neglected to realize the change of seasons. Timothy had come to understand what made humans so powerful. It was their magic, bound in spells and stories between the cover of books. Instructions on building traps, stories of adventure and justice. Words that once read, once believed, could manifest into reality.

By the time Timothy returned home to the mighty oak, his entire family was already there. He was wearing clothes, which wasn't unheard of for a mouse, but his fluffy white shirt and paperclip bent into the shape of a sword was probably a bit unusual and he was concerned how his brothers might tease him. It didn't matter. He wanted nothing more than to embrace his mother and tell her of all the adventures his mind had been on throughout the winter months. But something wasn't right upon returning home. The mighty oak tree which was just beginning to bloom and would normally be heavily populated with spring songbirds, was void of life and movement. There was an awful stillness across the entire prairie. Timothy's stomach sank and his heart began to pound. He ran to his home at the opening near the base of the mighty oak. In his horror, the entry to his home was torn wide and long trails of blood and entrails scattered the opening. The smell of death permeated from the tree. Timothy screamed for his mother. "Mom!" Nothing could be heard but a gentle breeze and then a distinctive sound that sent chills down Timothy's spine. The sound of wide large wings sweeping the air above.

Timothy looked up above to see not one, not two, but a parliament of owls covering the canopy of the tree. In that instance, he was torn between a primitive instinct to run and something deeper within him demanding to learn of what happened to his family. Before he could even process these thoughts, a shadow slowly grew from behind him, overtaking the landscape and he felt all the muscles of his body give way to pure terror. As he turned, he saw the figure of an owl with its wings raised up above its head. It seemed to fill the earth with its ever-expanding dimension. Timothy quickly pulled out his sword, which was a broken piece of a paperclip and held it up towards the owl. "Back beast!", he screamed loudly in a shrill voice. The owl paused and tilted its head, taking notice of the odd behavior.

Timothy summoned up the courage to scream again, "Where is my moth...". But before he could get the words out, a different owl had quietly swooped in and knocked the breath out of him, while clasping him in its talons. Timothy remembered being squeezed so tight that shortly after he could remember nothing at all.

When Timothy awoke to consciousness again, he was high up in the mighty oak tree. He instinctively attempted to stand to his feet, but the ground below him was soft and wet. It seemed to move with him as he attempted to stand. Nothing was left of his shirt except some loose rags dangling around his scratched and bloodied frame. As he slowly made his way to his feet, the reality of his situation slowly sank in. The loose ground on which he stood was the dismembered and mangled bodies of his brothers and sisters. Although he was not gravely injured, the sight of his family torn beneath his feet gave him the feeling of his bowels falling out from inside of him. He fell backwards stumbling away from the frightful pile of mice nestled into the fork of the mighty oak tree.

For Timothy the next few moments were difficult memories but also etched perfectly into his mind. As he lay there looking upon his loss, unable to grieve, yet completely overtaken by grief, he could feel all sense of hope draining from his body, as if he had a mortal wound and his blood was escaping him all at once, along with any instinct for survival. In a way, Timothy Gray died at that moment. And what was left, the shell of what he once was, began to fill with a boiling hot fury. The color returned to his cheeks, but life didn't return to his eyes. Instead, there rested a burning flame. Timothy turned to see an owl sitting proudly on its perch just a few limbs over from where he was. Timothy looked back at the pile of remains and saw there his bent metallic paperclip sword. Timothy slowly crawled back atop his family to retrieve the bit of wire he called a sword. He had only ever used it to practice on twigs and leaves. Even against such things, it did not prove very effective. He clutched the bent wire in his hand and rolled over on his back, unable to look any longer at the reality of the substrate on which he lay. He began to weep quietly as he gathered the courage to face his doom. Just as he began to sit up, he was stopped by a gentle hand on his shoulder.

Frightened at first, he turned quickly. It was his mother. She was barely recognizable from the last time he had seen her, battered and bruised. One hand extended out to Timothy, the other clutching the lifeless body of his baby sister Lilly. Timothy's eyes opened wide and he began to open his mouth to speak, but his mother quickly motioned her hand over her lips. "My dear Timothy" she began to weep, "You must go."

Timothy looked around with a quick glance, "Come, we will go together."

"I cannot, my legs are mangled." she motioned to her leg which had bone protruding. "You must go, son. Jump into the river and let the current take you far from here."

"I will not leave you", Timothy said, reaching out for her hand.

As she took him by the hand, both with tears running down their cheeks, unable to speak, Timothy set his sword down to better pull her to safety. Just then, a large burst of air nearly knocked him to the ground as an owl touched down directly in front of them both. The owl looked Timothy square in the eye and began lurching forward with its beak open wide. Timothy inched back but was frozen in fear. Suddenly, the owl let out the most horrific screech ever heard by mouse ears. Its head swung back to reveal Evelyn holding Timothy's blade steady in her hand, the blade sunken into the belly of the bird. Evelyn turned to Timothy and yelled "Run!" With that, the owl picked up its talon and slammed it into Evelyn's body, nearly running through completely. She collapsed as her body went limp. Timothy screamed, "No!"

The owl looked down at Evelyn's lifeless corpse. Feeling satisfied that she would not harm him again, the owl let out another loud shrill. The entire tree had now become alive with the beating of owl wings. Timothy rose to his feet and began to run down the length of a branch directly toward an owl flapping its wings. Owls are not accustomed to their prey running toward them. The owl began to fluff her chest and lifted her wings to attempt to intimidate Timothy. And Timothy did change his course, but not in a way the owl anticipated. Timothy ran up a divergent branch that was smaller and brought him dangerously close to the owl's sharp beak. As Timothy traveled down the length of the branch it began to bow downward, slowly taking him away from the owl and slowly stretching down until the angle was sharp enough that Timothy could just slide down the branch, grabbing onto the end and using the bounce in the tension of the lowering branch to launch himself into the air. The branch returned to wallop the owl directly under its still stretched out wing, tossing an explosion of feathers into the air. Timothy hit the water below and plunged deeply into the river. As he fought to find the surface, he quickly grew to question this decision, as mice are not excellent swimmers. Upon reaching the surface though, he was greeted by many delicate feathers floating atop the surface of the water.

This was the moment that Timothy learned that feathers

The Epic Of Timothy Gray

float. It was because of those few feathers that had gathered
on the water's surface, that he was able to coast with the
current away from the mighty oak that day, almost a year
ago, and today it is his boat of feathers that leads him back.
His boat had taken on some water, but he spread his weight
across the surface to stay afloat. Unsure if it is water from
the river or his own tears, running down his face, filling
his boat of feathers. Soon he will reach the forest side of
the river across from his old home. The area of the forest
the owls were have said to travel from and where he now
heads in search of justice, not as a young mouse afraid
and unprepared to fight, holding a paper clip, but like
magic books from his youth, he has planned and prepared
and returns now to exact cold and fearless revenge on the
creatures who took away his family. Armed now with a
weapon forged by the gods themselves and a will to fight that
matches its strength and resilience.

Chapter Three
Avoid Unnecessary Burdens

Timothy's feather raft was closely approaching the once distant shore on the forest edge. He began thrusting the reed into the deep waters attempting to catch the riverbed and adjust his course. His attempts were futile as the water was very deep and as Timothy leaned over the edge looking into the deep, he could only see his distorted reflection in the dark mirror of the water's surface. As he lowered the reed again as deeply as he could he felt it wobble in the water with a great deal of force. Timothy raised the stick again when suddenly the reed was dragged out of his hands, causing his boat to spin completely around. Disoriented and looking around him for where the reed went, he was only beginning to become aware of the frightening truth that he was not alone. He held his breath and attempted to minimize his movement, wanting to not draw more attention to himself.

The Epic Of Timothy Gray

He could see movement in the water around him but refrained from reacting, hoping that his raft would appear simply as refuse adrift.

He could see his destination ahead, all he had to do was drift a little farther, but the activity in the dark water around him was increasing and he could feel something hitting the side of his raft occasionally, causing him to spin faster still. The spinning caused him to lose his footing and stumble from one side of the boat to another. Suddenly the waters went silent as he could see the ripples from his movement spread across the water's surface. The hairs on the back of his head stood up as he sensed a rumble in the water approaching closer. Before he could fully process what was happening, the bottom of his raft lifted up and split into pieces, casting feathers, along with Timothy, out and away from what could only be described as a monstrous wide mouth bass with its mouth fully extended taking feather and grass into its cavity and then thrashing about half of its body extending out of the water.

Timothy found himself underwater, being pulled by an undercurrent, fighting to return to the surface. Mice can swim, but being submerged in water is a terrifying thing for a mouse and Timothy's fabric cape and belt holding his sword were only dragging him down. As he returned to the surface struggling to catch his breath, he grasped handfuls of water hoping to reach something that would aid his struggle. As he looked out across the water to get his bearings, he saw a frightfully large object coming straight for him. It was easily twice the size of the fish that broke his boat. He turned quickly and began fighting to reach the river's edge before being devoured by any beast of the deep. It was painfully obvious that the creature was gaining on him. He could hear the water being greatly disturbed behind him. He could not reach for his sword without risking sinking to the bottom. All hope was lost. He suddenly felt a pinch on his back, the cold water numbing him to the pain, he felt his body suddenly accelerate into the water in front of him. All he could do was hold his breath and cover his face from the force of water and violent thrashing behind him.

So it was a great surprise when Timothy felt his body lifted from the water. As he looked around to realize he was now on shore, he shook violently to free himself from his captor. He was tossed to the ground, wet and disheveled. This would be his opportunity now to make a stand against his foe. He drew his sword and jumped to his feet in one continuous motion. Not fully able to see the form before him with eyes still burning from the rushing water.

"Stand back foul beast!", Timothy bellowed while rubbing his eyes with one hand and pointing his blade with another. To his surprise, he saw a friendly face. Looking quite different, soaked with water, but with a very recognizable polite grin. It was Toby the opossum, whose grin turned timid at the sight of Timothy's sword. Timothy lowered his sword and inquired, "Tobias?"

"I am sorry sir, I am a curious soul, I didn't mean to intrude.

Were you going to battle the fish as well?" Toby asked apologetically.

"No, I am sorry, I appreciate your assistance." Timothy re-sheathed his sword and took a deep breath. "I honestly thought I had met the end of my story there. I have never been fond of water. I always feel like no matter how hard I swim, I will never escape it." Timothy said, his head sinking low in shame.

"Oh, I love a good swim, I do." Toby said with a large smile. "I swim this river every day, sometimes twice a day."

"How very admirable and impressive. I am indebted to you sir." Timothy said with a gentleman's bow.

"You are a funny mouse. I like the way you talk." Toby said with admiration.

"As much as I appreciate your accolades, I must be on my way. You should head home." Timothy said looking at the sky which was beginning to glow, showing signs of an approaching sunrise. As he turns to walk away he can hear Toby mutter, "Well, I don't really have a home."

"Oh, I'm sorry to hear that. Was your home lost?" Timothy remembered his childhood home to which he has never returned.

Toby, realizing the touchy subject he had approached,

responded, "No, no, my home is wherever I lay my head. I have never been good at building a nest and I just feel safer when I am on the move."

"Yes, I can understand that. I have also adapted to living a life on the run. Although it does not make me feel safe at all. Instead, I feel as though I am constantly under threat of attack. Danger seems to loom at every turn, and I am but a tantalizing morsel to most of the creatures I run into. I am honestly surprised you have not yet attempted to devour me." Timothy said, giving an accusing glance at Toby's large grin of sharp teeth.

Toby just leaned in with wide eyes and said "I sure do like the way you talk."

Timothy did not appear pleased with Toby's response to his inquiry.

Toby looked around slightly embarrassed. "To tell you the truth, I do not enjoy hairy flesh. I never much have. Rarely get the opportunity anyway. With the exception of your owl friend back there, it has been weeks since I have eaten anything that wasn't brought up from the earth."

"That feathered beast was no friend of mine." Timothy said in disgust. Suddenly a loud, almost deafening, screech came from nearby, just downstream from their position. Both Timothy and Toby cowered instinctively at the loud shrill sound and then looked at each other.

"Follow me, I know a nearby log we can hide in." Toby whispered quietly and began walking backwards away from the sound slowly. Sounds echoed through the early morning air of a struggle in the distance. Again, a deep honking howl ripped through the air and was almost painful to Timothy and Toby's ears. This time the loud honking was mixed with a sharp white noise, like rain on the old tin roof of the hunting lodge.

Timothy reached for his sword and began walking toward the sound. "Where are you going?" Toby raised his voice in concern. Timothy turned to Toby, "Yes, you should seek safety. I am on a path that you can not follow." Timothy turned back to the direction where the continued piercing screech resonated and began quietly stepping through the tall grass, avoiding contact with underbrush so as to not give away his position. Toby pondered for a moment but felt a great deal of concern mixed with curiosity over his new friend. "Timothy...", he called out, stepping forward to follow. "Friend, wait, what if death awaits you as it does that creature who cries?"

Timothy turned to see Toby shoving his way through the brush. He let out a slow breath of disappointment. "Toby, sir, you cannot follow this path. Plus, you are not exactly a creature of discrete stride." Timothy looked up at the obvious division of grass where Toby stood.

"But, friend, we do not know what dangers lie beyond in that scuffle down there. This is a dangerous time of morning to venture out."

Timothy paused and looked down. Then he raised his head calmly remembering a poem he had once read of the old Greek warriors and he spoke softly,

"And how can man die better
Than facing fearful odds,
For the ashes of his fathers,
And the temples of his Gods,"

A peaceful but crazed smile came across Timothy's face, "You must stay behind, or you will give away my position. Worry not for me, for I go to chop at the root of evil. That is the cry of suffering, I know it well. If death awaits me there, then all the better for me. You should find shelter. You are a noble creature and your company has lifted my spirits, but I can not carry more burden than I already do. Goodbye again friend."

With that, Timothy turned and darted into the underbrush, weaving into the shadows. Toby looked to the ground, his heart heavy. "I am not a burden", he muttered and lowered his head and turned his head to walk away.

Chapter Four
Misery Loves Company

Timothy reached a small clearing and the source of the violent cries. He hid in the brush to assess the situation. A rather large goose with its wings stretched high was waving about in a threatening manner, ducking and weaving as if it was in a territorial dispute with another bird. Timothy looked around to see who this goose was ready to do battle with. That is when he heard a sound that instinctively made him cower to the ground. It was like that of the rain on the tin roof, but now closer, it was intense and distinct, and that is when Timothy saw it. Just past the goose in a small crevasse in the terrain was the tail of a snake and on the end a large rattle almost half the size of Timothy himself. It shook so fierce that it became almost invisible as the sharp sound caused both the goose and Timothy to recoil and cover their ears.

The Epic Of Timothy Gray

Timothy, who had spent the last year training himself to face his fears head on now felt inside him a terror he had never experienced before. Something generations deep in his soul told him to run and hide. Maybe Toby was right and he was a fool for rushing into such an unknown enemy. Timothy decided to climb the brush and get a better perspective on the size of the snake.

Upon reaching the top of a curled branch of a bush Timothy was able to see and comprehend the full terror of the situation. The snake was coiled and twisted, making it impossible to gauge its full size, but what really struck at Timothy's heart was to see the snake with its jaws stretched wide devouring a young gosling.. It was struggling to get the small bird past its jaws while looking at the mother goose right in the eyes. The goose was still shrieking in a loud slurry of sound, a blend of terror, anger and remorse. The situation was impossible. Timothy had never encountered such an enemy and with only moments to decide a course of action, he deeply considered the possibility that it was too late. He also began balancing his own mission for justice with this goose's cry for help. He closed his eyes and pressed his head against the vine he held to. His mind was drawn to a letter he had once read in a newspaper clipping, his friend Philip the pack rat had kept cherished in his nest. "An injustice anywhere is an injustice everywhere", Timothy would often struggle with concepts of justice and ethical righteousness in a world fraught with violence and despair. Do the men who write such words face such snakes as this? Timothy pondered to himself.

The loud scuffle of flapping wings and continued rattling
pulled Timothy back into the moment. Timothy could
see that the snake had now devoured the gosling and was
positioning itself to strike against the goose who was still
flailing about in an attempt to scare the snake away. That
is when Timothy first noticed, cowered behind the mother
goose was another baby gosling, just barely a hatchling.
When Timothy saw the look of fear on the baby gosling who
had just witnessed the murder of its sibling, he no longer
needed to weigh the decision. Timothy sprang into action.
He lunged forward and positioned himself in front of the last
remaining gosling and drew his sword. The mother goose,
unsure of his motivation, turned to him still screaming
at the top of her lungs, almost insane now with fear and
dread. "I am here to assist you madam." Timothy said as
he stepped toward the snake taking its attention away from
the Goose and now solely onto him. The goose, realizing the
opportunity, began backing away and pushing its remaining
young from the nest and away from the clearing.

"What gives you the right to take the life of another?"
Timothy yelled out in anger.

The snake, still struggling to swallow down the first gosling,
looked down on Timothy with wide eyes and an awkward
grin. "Take a life?", the snake responded with a hiss. "I have
never taken anything that wasn't offered up freely by the
weaker among us." The snake drew closer to Timothy and
looked him in the eyes. The glands on his face fluctuated
as he smelled Timothy. "I only kill what I need to survive.

Nothing more. Can you say the same, odd little mouse?"
Timothy looked down at his blood stained hair and clothes.
The rattlesnake pulled its head away from Timothy and again
forcing its meal farther down its body it spoke, "Perhaps you
should not be lecturing others about taking a life."

Timothy turned to see that the goose and gosling were now
far away. He was now alone. His nerves obviously affected by
standing before such a large snake, which had now stopped
rattling and was slowly unraveling and seemed to grow in
size by the second. The sword in Timothy's hand began to
shake as the snake rose in stature until his head blocked out
the rising sun peaking through the peaks of the tall grass.
"I wish you had arrived before my meal, I prefer the taste
of rodents." said the snake, extending its jaw open wide to
display its elongated fangs.

Timothy began stepping backwards to put some space
between him and the intimidating snake, but the snake,
almost as if floating on air, began descending toward him.
Hissing at Timothy with his long forked tongue, "I am afraid
though, I can not let you, a pathetic field mouse, walk away
after challenging me in such a contemptible way. It would be
an affront to the very order of everything."

"I warn you. You may strike me down, but at great cost. This
blade in my hand is no meager weapon. It was given to me
by the gods to smite the likes of you!" Timothy spoke boldly,
somewhat from his heart, but also stalling. Knowing full well
that a strike from a rattler's venom is a death sentence.

The snake took pause at these words and looked closer upon the blade held by a field mouse. It was all just odd enough to take notice and warrant concern. Timothy's blade shone reflecting the rising sun and the snake winced at the shimmering light. Timothy took notice of the snake's sensitivity to the reflected light and turned his sword to place a reflective shimmer on the snake's eyes. It reared its head back and diverted its gaze for a moment. Timothy turned and ran as quickly as he could, but the snake was determined now. The snake flung itself forward in pursuit. Timothy turned to see the snake closing the gap between them and preparing to strike, its head raised up and fangs exposed hissing in anger.

Timothy turned to make his last stand, spreading his cape wide with one hand hoping to confuse the snake and his sword stretched out in the other. The snake raised its head and spread its jaws wide. Just as Timothy braced himself to receive a deadly blow, the snake suddenly recoiled in pain and the rattle that had gone quiet now shot straight up in the air and was shaking so violently that the sound was deafening. The snake and Timothy both turned their head to the snake's lower portion where just a few inches from the rattle stood a dirty white haired opossum named Toby with a mouth full of snake butt and an oddly satisfying grin on his face.

The snake quickly reared its head back and struck Toby just above his right shoulder.

The Epic Of Timothy Gray

"No!" Timothy shouted, charging forward.

Toby bit down harder, the snake now writhing in pain turned to strike him a second time. This time it struck him in the back and held tight. Toby winced but ever more determined began grinding his teeth sawing through snake flesh. Timothy lunged onto the snake's mid-section just above where it was digesting the baby gosling and plunged his sword deep into the snake. The snake released Toby who had now almost completely severed the rattler tail from the snake and the rattle had ceased vibrating and was now just twitching on the ground. The snake coiled more, trapping Timothy in its folds. Timothy being tumbled into a twisted maze of scaled muscle was feeling the crush on his body. He had no escape, but hand still on the sword he pressed down. With every press of the sword he felt the grip of the snake grow weaker. The snake unraveled exposing Timothy to the sunlight and there above him was the snake looking prepared to strike. Timothy, having no way out, looked to the opening he had carved in the snake's abdomen and being desperate for shelter did something no mouse would ever willingly do. He crawled into the belly of the snake. The snake upon seeing this became outraged and struck at him, sinking his fangs into his own flesh. Timothy lay curled inside of the snake's stretched out belly with a dead bird to his left and fangs poking through the flesh directly in front of him, dripping a deadly toxin.

As the snake drew back to strike again he saw a blade

burst out of his own flesh, causing him to jerk and twitch involuntarily. The blade would retract and then burst through from another position. The snake hissed violently, eyes wide with horror and opened its mouth wide, extending his fangs out as far as he could stretch them, but before he could strike he felt the sharp grasp of Toby wrapping his jaws around his neck, just below his head, leaving him immobile. Toby pulled his head down low to the ground and he was forced to watch as a mouse carved through his abdomen and crawled out covered in blood. The snake's body continued squirming and fighting almost involuntarily as Toby tugged and bit down hard. The sound of bones cracking beneath his powerful jaws. Timothy was now face to face with the snake.

"What kind of devil are you?" The snake whispered as it grew weaker from the struggle. Timothy, exhausted and struggling to catch his breath, looked up at the snake and responded, "I am but a mouse in possession of the magic of men. Magic that tells of a snake which deceives. I am no devil. I have come to give the devil his due." Timothy looked Toby in the eye and gave him a nod as he approached the snake and placed his hand upon the snake's broad nose. "Consider this a mercy.", Timothy spoke as he quickly dove his sword deep into the eye of the snake. The snake convulsed and flailed around one last time. Timothy withdrew his sword and breathed deeply before looking at Toby, still holding the neck of the snake in his mouth. Toby gently released the snake and it collapsed to the ground. Then Toby fell and his arm began to twitch on the side where he had been bitten. Timothy dropped his sword and ran to his aid and attempted to help pick him up. But Toby was far too large and he was barely able to lift his arm. "Sir Toby, why ever would you do that?", Timothy said sorrowfully.

Toby said softly, "I wanted to show you. I am not a burden."

"You most definitely are not a burden friend." Timothy's eyes welled up with tears as he embraced Toby, or at least as much of him as he could. Timothy whispered, "That is twice now that you have saved my life in as little time as I have known you. You sir are a gentle knight among creatures. A hero if ever there was one."

"I am very tired Timothy", said Toby, "and cold."

Timothy wrapped his arms wide and attempted to comfort him. "It is alright, friend. Rest comfortably. I will not leave your side." Timothy nuzzled his head into Toby's side and although overwhelmed with grief, he felt very much safe and at peace. The two of them, both worn and exhausted, drifted to sleep in the warmth of the sun.

A large shadow loomed over them as they slept.

Chapter Five

Chosen By The Gods

Timothy awoke buried deep in a bed of soft moss and luxuriously soft down feathers. He rubbed his eyes for a moment. It had been a long time since Timothy had slept that well and he was a bit confused about his current situation. He began to realize that his robe and belt had been removed. He quickly turned in a panic realizing his sword wasn't on him. There next to him laid his clothes, belt, sword and all, neatly folded and just within reach. He looked up to see a giant goose that was stretching its head down to eye level. "I took the liberty of washing your things down in the river. I hope you don't mind, but I did not want blood in my nest.", said the towering goose in an odd quivering voice. Timothy had not spoken to a goose before. The cold reality is that he had not spoken to many creatures apart from Philip and his family. After the dark day at the mighty oak tree

The Epic Of Timothy Gray

Timothy returned to the only place he felt safe, the hunting lodge. And there he buried himself in books. Everything in the outside world only reminded him of what he had lost, but in those stories, he was able to forget, if only for a moment.

"Why do you wear these things?", the goose's question pulled him back into the moment. Timothy began putting on his wardrobe which consisted of a cape made from a gentleman's handkerchief and a leather belt and sheath cut from the thumb of an old discarded sheepskin work glove. Tucked into his belt on either side were two fingertips of a glove a longer one used as a sheath for his sword and a shorter one that he would use as a pocket for seeds that he carried for food on his journey.

"It is a bit odd. Do you think yourself a man?", she poked again.

"Madam...", he began to answer the question, but then realized a greater concern, "How did I get here?" Timothy was sitting in an obviously used nest and by the look of the brown coloration of the down feathers from which it was composed, he was likely speaking to the owner of the nest.

"My husband and I brought you and your friend over to keep a watchful eye on you while you slept. It was the least we could do after what you both did for my sister Mary."

Suddenly Timothy felt as if all the blood had been drained

from his body as he was reminded of the events of that morning. "Oh no, Toby! Where is my friend, the white opossum, he is dying!"

"Dying you say?" a gander came stumbling onto the scene. He had a silly grin on his face and chuckled as he spoke, "Well that is the healthiest dying opossum I have ever seen." Timothy gave him a confused look. The gander waddled closer and stretched out his wing to Timothy, "Climb up, I will take you to your friend."

As Timothy climbed up on the gander's wing he was lifted high into the air. Suddenly he could see above the underbrush and all the way to the river. He was in awe of how many birds he could see, their long necks poking out of the tall grass. Now he could hear them as well, a flood of chatter and squeaking filled the air. He climbed down to the gander's shoulder. "There are so many of you." Timothy spoke with a sense of wonder.

"Yes, we nest here, but we will travel to good feeding grounds as soon as the goslings are ready for flight. Speaking of goslings, I think I see your friend."

Timothy looked down to see Toby with a gosling riding on his back, jumping around like a wild stallion. The gander made his way toward them and pointed his wing to the ground. Timothy slid down his wing and ran up to Toby who was smiling and bouncing around while the gosling on his back giggled and honked. They both froze upon making eye contact. Timothy was confused and Toby slightly embarrassed to be playing like a child.

"Toby, I don't understand, I saw the rattler strike you." Timothy said concerned.

"Oh yeah, it really hurt, but I feel better now." Toby said with indifference.

"But I was always taught that a rattler's blow was a death sentence." Timothy said, still confused.

"Maybe we shouldn't talk about you know what in front of you know who." Toby said, gesturing his eyes to the gosling still bouncing on his back.

The gander lowered his head into their conversation, "Yes, that reminds me, Mary will want to thank you personally." He lowered his wing out to Timothy again.

The gosling on Toby's back spoke up, "Mommy?"

Toby quickly diverted, "Mommy is still tired little Dorothy, let's go hunt for grubs. I think I saw a juicy one over here." Toby smiled and the gosling giggled and spoke, "Yummy in my tummy!"

"Yes, yummy grubs. We can gather some for mother Mary

too" Toby said cheerfully as they hopped away.

As Timothy climbed onto the gander's shoulder again the gander whispered, "Dorothy isn't quite aware of what all took place this morning." He turned and began walking to the clearing where other geese circled around quietly where a small goose lay on the nest where they did battle with the snake. "Mary had lost her husband to a pack of wild dogs just before Daniel and Dorothy were hatched. I am afraid the loss of Daniel may have pushed her over the edge. Just be aware, she is a good goose. She is just still in shock."

"I understand." Timothy spoke before fully grasping the situation.

The gander lowered Timothy down to the ground in front of Mary, who was cradling the limp colorless body of a dead gosling. She was rocking him and singing a gentle song. Timothy's eyes diverted to the floor which still showed evidence of the struggle earlier that day. He could see in the distance the mangled and dismembered body of the snake.

"Mary, this is the brave mouse who rescued you." The gander looked down at Timothy, "What was your name brave mouse?"

Timothy cleared his throat, "Timothy, Timothy Gray.

Mary looked up and stretched her neck down until she was

eye to eye with Timothy.

"Thank you Timothy, thank you for saving my precious family." Mary spoke softly with a quiet reluctance.

"You are most welcome my lady." Timothy instinctively bowed down, somewhat confused about how to respond.

Mary lifted the lifeless corpse of her gosling and nuzzled it with her beak. "If you hadn't stepped in, I may have lost my baby boy."

Timothy's eyes grew wide. The circle of geese all looking away from the horror of what Mary was going through. "I only did what anyone else would do."

Mary began rocking and singing again looking straight into the face of her dead child. "Let us give her some space." Said the gander and he brushed Timothy onto his wing. As they turned to walk away Timothy let out a long slow breath. "Poor thing.", Timothy spoke in a whisper.

"Grief can make people do strange things." said the gander with an air of sage wisdom.

"Yes, I am familiar." Timothy said coldly, staring off into space with what he had just seen weighing heavy in his heart.

"You know, what you did was not what anyone would do.

Sure, for one of your own, maybe. But for another kind, it is a rare thing to bear witness to in this forest." The gander said inquisitively.

"We all bleed the same. Are we not of the same kind?" Timothy contemplated as he considered Philip, who he grew to accept as family despite their differences in appearance. And now his thoughts went to Toby. "I must speak with my companion, the white opossum."

"Of course, Tobias Greenbottom" The gander said with a chuckle.

"You know Toby?" asked Timothy.

"Oh, I have run into him in the past. He normally keeps to himself. It is just his name that makes me laugh. Surely that cannot be a family name." The gander pondered as they walked along. Timothy did not comprehend, but smiled and pretended to understand the humor, hoping it was not at the expense of his new friend.

"Here we are.", the gander lowered Timothy down as they came to an opening where Toby and the baby gosling were picking through an old rotted tree limb on the ground, eating the grubs and insects. Timothy walked up and picked a snail off the tree limb, lifted up to his mouth and sucked the slimy insides right out of the shell. He then groaned in pleasure, "These are my favorite."

The Epic Of Timothy Gray

The small gosling waddled up to Timothy with her wings full of grubs and larvae, gesturing as if to offer him some.

"Little Dorothy, this is my friend, Timothy Gray", Toby said proudly.

The baby gosling looked Timothy in the eye and spoke, "Timmy Dee Dee Gway".

Toby smiled from ear to ear and looked at Timothy.

"Come little one, let us take those treats to your mother." said the gander, giving Timothy a moment with his friend.

As she waddled away with the gander, Toby turned again to Timothy with a very large grin. "Timmy Dee Dee!" as he broke out in a giggle. "How adorable is that?"

Timothy nodded, mildly amused but also wanting to ask Toby a serious question.

"Toby, friend, comrade... brother. I am on a quest. An assignment given to me by the gods." Timothy rambled.

Toby drew a serious face.

"I do not believe that as I just began my journey that I stumbled upon you by accident. You who swam so well when I was in danger. You who fought so bravely when I was in peril. You who received two lashes of the rattles fang, but still here you stand. I do not believe this to be a coincidence." Timothy looked up to the sky.

"Toby, I believe the gods are calling to you as they called to me when they gifted me with my blade." Timothy continued as Toby's serious face was returning to a big goofy grin.

"Toby, would you join me on my quest to the deep woods in search of justice for my family?" Timothy asked with his chest held high.

"You sure I'm not a burden?" Said Toby timidly.

"No brother, You are a true hero. A champion. I am sorry that I at all considered you a burden." Timothy said contritely.

"Well, I guess I could go on a quest. I have never been on one before." Toby answered, a little confused about the details, but Toby had tasted adventure now with Timothy, and it made him feel an energy he had never experienced before. Like a delicious fruit fallen to the ground perfectly ripe, he had tasted it and could not bring himself to walk away.

"Good to hear brother, let us take the day to forage and get well rested. We will depart for the deep forest tonight when the moon is high above." Timothy spoke, and then placing a hand on Toby's shoulder said sincerely, "I am ever so glad you are okay Toby."

Toby made a serious face and responded. "Me too Timmy Dee Dee", as he broke into laughter. Timothy smiled, which was not an expression he was completely comfortable with, but Toby had a trouble free spirit that was beginning to grow on Timothy. They spent the rest of the day and into the evening feasting on grubs, nuts and berries and enjoying the company of the geese whose towering presence provided both shelter from predators and a sense of family belonging that they both deeply enjoyed. All the while, Toby sharing stories of their brave travels and letting slip their intended journey through the deep forest.

The gosling, upon overhearing Toby's dramatic story telling, leaned in toward Timothy and whispered, "your journey may find enlightenment if you consult the soul of the forest."

"The soul of the forest?" Timothy asked inquisitively.

The gosling appeared to look around as if such things were not meant to be shared with all. "I have never met him myself, but I hear great things, you know, in the breeze. Ask any winged friend and they may be so obliged to guide your way, for we are the ones who carry the breeze to the soul of the forest, it is an arrangement as old as time. The soul can guide you on your adventure, I will make sure of it and make way your path."

"I appreciate your insight my tall friend, and I will seek out this one you call the soul of the forest. But how, may I ask, will you make way my path?" Timothy asked politely.

"I will whisper your name in the breeze, Timothy. Honestly, with as much as your friend Tobias has shared, I need not say a word. Geese are a gossipy foul. But our gaggle owes you dearly, so trust me, we will whisper your name into the breeze such that all will come to know of the mouse, his sword, and his brave companion."

"Thank you." Timothy said with an unsure gratitude. Not fully understanding how gossiping geese would help him in his journey. With that, they all nestled down for an evening nap.

The Epic Of Timothy Gray

Chapter Six
The Twisted Forest

The night was cool and the waxing moon above made the
blades of grass glow with a soft blue hue. Toby was sleeping
snug between a goose and the young gosling Dorothy.
Timothy walked softly up to the group who was sleeping
soundly and began tugging on Toby's tail. Toby awoke
and his deep warm smile dissolved into a puzzled glare at
Timothy. "It is time", Timothy said softly as he tip towed
away from the twisted nest of sleeping birds. Toby slowly
stood up and followed before quickly returning to push
Dorothy up close with another goose so she would stay
warm.

The two set off toward the forest edge. "Timothy, what is
it we hope to find in the forest at night?" Toby whispered.
The forest trees intertwined with vines and the underbrush

to create a porous wall of life. The very sight of which discouraged most prairie creatures from entering.

"Just beyond the forest, if legend is true, is the breeding grounds for the long eared owls who brutally attacked the mighty oak tree and killed my family." Timothy said with a smoldering rage.

"And once we find these owls, what then?" Toby inquired, worried that he didn't want to hear the answer.

"I want answers. I want to know why they went mad that day. And once I have my answers, I want them all to know suffering as I have. And I shall carve them through with my steel until they have come to know it well." Timothy said while stepping through vines and crossing into the forest floor. Toby followed, looking around cautiously. "Yes, I also have many questions about the days of thunder. Strange times indeed." Toby said while struggling to keep up with Timothy's resolute pace. Timothy stopped in his tracks and turned to face Toby. "What do you mean, days of thunder?"

"Oh, you know how the forest breeze carries whispers of stories. That is what we have come to call it. The day preceding the great migration. When the creatures of the deep woods came into the prairie in unusual numbers. This is the day that the mighty oak was attacked, as well as many others." Toby said as he looked down to the ground. "I am surprised you have not heard others speak of it."

Timothy felt a great deal of shame, "I have been away from the prairie for a long while."

"Oh, well little is known really, but many say that they heard the air crack with thunder, but the sky was clear that day. Some say it was an omen and I have heard stories like it from all over." Toby said feeling very smart. "I don't remember hearing it myself. But I felt it. The earth shifted and nearly collapsed my home." Toby paused for a moment, recalling the trauma of that day and how that was the last time he called someplace home. He continued, "It was awful. I was so scared. It was like every animal left the forest that day and I nearly got trampled." He paused for a moment, remembering how this was also the day that he met Timothy's mother, but decided not to mention it, as he didn't want to bring forth difficult memories. "We were all scared that day. No one knew what happened, but we were all scared." Toby spoke solemnly.

Timothy placed a hand on Toby's shoulder as a gesture of support and then turned and began marching onward into the woods. "We will find our answers", Timothy pressed on into the forest, "and I will have my justice."

The forest floor was thick with brush and the ground was soft with layers of decay and death. Timothy had noticed the smell had shifted as they entered deeper into the forest. Everything smelled of earth and mushrooms. The cicada bugs were singing loudly in waves of harmonics that seemed to oscillate from tree to tree. Timothy walked, lifting his head up frequently, keeping an eye toward the trees for signs of danger. Toby, quite the opposite, sniffed the ground and at moments seemed to walk blindly into the brush attempting to smell his way through the night. The bright moon above provided plenty of light, poking its way through the hanging canopy onto the floor below. Timothy could make out the shapes of the trees above. He could see the occasional shape of what could be a bird, but nothing much larger than himself.

"When I was young, I was taught never to enter the woods. These are the prime hunting grounds for all manner of creatures. Yet it seems peaceful and quiet." Timothy said wearily as he turned to see that Toby was no longer behind him.

"Toby!?" Timothy whispered as he cowered down in fear. "Toby, where did you go?"

"I'm over here." Toby bellowed out from behind a nearby tree. Timothy rushed to his friend to see him standing in a thick pile of leaves with a confused look on his face.

"Toby, we must stay together", Timothy said as he breathed a deep breath of relief. Toby had his nose buried in the ground sniffing.

"Timothy, I found something strange", Toby said as he

stretched his hand out into the leaves and pushed forth out of the brown decaying pile a brightly colored blue egg. Timothy grew concerned. "Toby, don't touch it. Perhaps its owner is nearby." as he looked around cautiously. "This could be the egg of a forest beast. What if this is the egg of a rattler? We should keep moving." Timothy said with a false air of confidence.

"Timothy, rattlers don't lay eggs." Toby said with a chuckle, "And this smells like a bird's nest."

"How do you know such things?" Timothy inquired.

"Well, to be completely honest, yesterday was not my first taste of a rattler." Toby said, mildly ashamed. "And even you should know what a bird nest smells like."

Timothy leaned in and smelled the egg. It did remind him of the goose nest. He looked at Toby and then they both looked up above them into the tree. Sure enough, there was a nest not too far from them in the tree above. They both then looked back down and made eye contact. Timothy motioned his hands down the path into the forest. "We are on a quest Toby", he pleaded.

Toby looked down at the egg and then back up at Timothy. "Maybe this is also our quest?" Toby asked gently. Timothy looked down the path and then back up at the nest and then down the path again. "Alright Toby, how do you propose we return this hatchling back to its nest?"

"I can climb trees very well, but I fear if I grasp the egg in my mouth, I could end up accidentally eating it." Toby said while tapping the egg with his claw.

"Perhaps together we can solve this problem." Timothy said while looking around the forest. He pulled his knife from his belt and walked toward the tree trunk. He sliced off a piece of vine that was growing up the tree. He pulled on it, following it to where it came up from the ground. He then sliced it at the base and sheathed his sword. He coiled the vine around one hand and began pulling off the small leaves from it.

"Just how good are you at climbing?" Timothy asked, weighing his idea for a solution.

"Oh, I rarely fall." Toby said confidently. Timothy's reaction was not comforted by the use of the word rarely.

Timothy began twisting the vine into a knot. "I am going to put this around you." He warned while placing the vine around Toby's midsection. "You will climb the tree, and I will hold the egg. Once it is returned to the nest, we can make haste. We don't want to be in the forest when the sun comes up." Timothy said while picking up the egg. He climbed onto Toby's back and tucked himself into the harness he had crafted from the vine that was tied around Toby's chest. Toby smiled with excitement. "Ready when you are sir." Timothy said fearfully, clutching the egg in one arm and grasping the vine with the other.

Toby slowly made his way to the tree trunk and then began climbing the tree. He stretched out his sharp claws and dug them into the bark of the tree while wrapping his tail around the trunk as far as it would reach. Taking turns between pushing with his tail and pulling with his outstretched arms, Toby ascended the trunk of the tree. For Toby, it was a smooth and gentle climb up the tree. Timothy, on the other hand, shifted and shook with every repositioning of Toby's body. Timothy tucked the egg under his chin so that it wouldn't come loose during the long bouncy climb up. As they approached the branch that contained the nest, Timothy's arms grew tired of holding the vine that was slowly becoming looser with the climb. "I think that is close enough." He said as he wiggled out from the vine and onto the branch below them.

Timothy walked the egg out on the branch carefully, avoiding looking down to the ground below and focussing on the nest ahead. When he reached the nest, he could see that there were inside the nest two baby blue birds with bright orange beaks sleeping curled up together half buried with straw and grass. They looked quite peaceful and cute, thought Timothy. He reached forward and gently laid the egg beside them in the nest. The tiny baby birds seemed to move slightly as if to notice the presence of the egg, but their eyes were not yet open. Timothy turned to Toby with a smile and a sense of accomplishment. Then a small chirp sound came from the nest. Timothy turned to see a baby bird stretching its neck out of the nest and opening its mouth as if it was yawning. "Chirp" he heard again, thinking it was somewhat cute. Then again. Now both baby birds sat up chirping profusely. Timothy began to grow concerned and started walking backwards away from the nest, trying to hush the babies. "Shhhh, It's alright." Suddenly a blue jay darted downward and onto the nest, touching the babies as if to count them. It then looked down at the egg in the nest and then up to make eye contact with Timothy. "Madam, we simply wanted to..." before Timothy could get the next word out the blue jay screeched loudly and then darted towards Timothy who was taken completely by surprise. The blue jay jabbed and pecked at Timothy who was not able to keep his footing while defending himself from the bird's attack. Timothy fell from the tree before Toby could reach for him. The blue jay turned its attack toward Toby who was trying to look down to where Timothy had fallen. Timothy hit the ground with a thud. Toby lifted his hands in defense as the blue jay continued its assault, pecking and flapping its wings in a fury. Toby out of frustration let out a large hiss and opened his mouth wide showing rows of jagged sharp teeth. The blue jay backed away instinctively giving Toby a moment to escape down the tree quickly as he fumbled down the trunk of the tree clawing the branches and trunk to slow his descent. The blue bird took off into the air and began making dive runs past Toby.

Timothy rose up from the ground with dead leaves and forest floor moss stuck to his back. He shook the debris off, but the pain of his fall made him pause to stretch out his joints slowly. He began feeling up and down his body for signs of injury and then it hit him. His sword was gone. It must have been separated from him when he hit the ground. The blue bird kept swinging low and causing Toby to duck to the ground and hiss in return. Toby had made it to the floor but was having a hard time getting to Timothy while under constant assault from the blue jay. Timothy was frantically looking around for his sword, tossing up the forest floor contemplating how it might have fallen. Timothy looked to Toby, "I lost my sword!"

"Perhaps this is more an opportunity for diplomacy anyway?" Toby responded becoming weary of the blue jay's constant attack runs. "We were simply trying to help!" Toby screamed at the blue jay. Timothy looked down for his sword again. Through the constant cawing, as it continued to set off alarms for the entire forest to hear, there could be heard a distinctly different call. A call that caused all three creatures, Timothy, Toby, and the blue jay to pause and turn their heads. It called out again. "kee-eeeee-arr". They heard a war cry that sent shivers down their collective spines. The blue jay instantly vanished back into her nest. Toby turned to Timothy as Timothy quietly mouthed, "Hawk." with wide eyes and lips trembling in fear.

Quickly they ran to the underbrush to seek cover in the thorned vines and bushes on the forest floor. Toby was struggling to get comfortable surrounded by the thorns and thistles. Timothy leaned against the vines to keep an eye out for his lost weapon. "Do you think we are safe here?" asked Toby.

"For the moment, but I must get to my blade." Timothy said frustrated. "It is our only hope of success in all of this."

Toby, finding a comfortable position, inquired "Can you simply ask the gods for another one?"

"I don't think it works like that Toby. We are gifted one chance in this life." Timothy responded fervently while still peering out onto the forest floor for any sign of his sword.

"How does it work Timothy? How did the gods give it to you in the first place?" Toby asked rather irreverently with a mild apprehension toward myth and fairytale.

Timothy paused his search and turned to Toby. "It is a long story."

"I do like a story." Toby said bashfully.

Timothy turned to see a glimmer of light in the corner of his eye. In the distance, a small shard of steel stuck out of the forest floor and just perfectly reflected the moonlight. "I see it.", Timothy exclaimed. He turned his head to look down the path. There was a hedge of honeysuckle that extended for as far as he could see. "Toby, I think we should make a break for it. To that bush of honeysuckle just down the path."

Toby was reluctant, but as he attempted to look down the

path he was scratched yet again by the thorn of the vine and quickly decided that honeysuckle would make a much more pleasant long term hideout. "Okay Timothy, I am ready when you are." Toby said in a firm whisper.

Timothy had not averted his gaze from the glimmer of light that could be his sword, "I will go first and reach my sword. You head straight for the honeysuckle", Timothy said while stepping out from the vines and briefly looking above for signs of danger. He gave a few quick glances to the tree line and then sprinted at full step toward his sword. Toby struggled to wiggle free from the thorn bush. Once he was free he could see Timothy was already diving to the ground to retrieve his sword. Toby took off toward the safety of the honeysuckle bushes. Toby was not gifted with great speed or light footing. The faster he attempted to run the harder he seemed to waddle, shifting his weight from side to side.

Timothy reached the sword quickly and slid to the ground gracefully grabbing the handle and pulling it from the soil. It was caked with dirt at the tip, but otherwise in perfect condition. Timothy looked up to see Toby's back end shaking as he ran. Timothy bolted in pursuit and they both reached the safety of cover at the same time. There was no sign of the hawk. The forest was quiet. They were each catching their breath when Timothy postulated, "perhaps the hawk was after another prey?"

Toby turned to see Timothy who had dropped to his knees

and was holding his sword out to inspect it. Timothy began cleaning the dirt off and using his cape to polish the steel. "Timothy, perhaps we should lie low for a moment to ensure the hawk is gone", Toby suggested.

Timothy nodded, still buffing and shining the steel of his blade. "That is probably a good idea."

"Maybe you can tell me the story while we wait. The story of how the gods gifted you this weapon." Toby asked in a whisper as he drove his body into the ground cover almost as if to snuggle up for a bedtime story. Timothy leaned back and looked at Toby who had a grin of anticipation. "I will attempt to explain, but then we must set forth, we have much ground to cover."

Timothy held his sword up so that it reflected and glistened in the moonlight and began to gently tell his tale.

"Once long ago in the world of men, there lived a young man who became king of all men. He was guided on his journey to a lake, where a mysterious woman gifted him a sword. Not just any sword, but one with mystical powers. The sword was called Excalibur."

Toby's jaw was drooping open. "Mystical powers?" he whispered in amazement, really enjoying the opportunity to hear a story.

Timothy sat up and continued, "Yes, well, I once read

this account of human history in a book, a container of human spells, strong human magic, which I had assumed only worked on humans. But then the fateful day at the mighty oak." Timothy became lost in his own thoughts for a moment, "on that day, I nearly drowned in the river upon my escape. When I washed up on shore, I was a dead mouse. My heart felt like it had been ripped out of me. I had nothing and no one. When I looked out upon the shallow waters where I awoke, I saw a shimmering light rising up out of the waters. I reached in the water and from it I pulled this." Timothy held his blade to Toby so he could see. "It reads on the side, X-ACTO, followed by the number 10."

Toby looked over the engraving carefully, but did not know what it said. "What does that mean?" Toby asked.

"X-ACTO is my Excalibur. The women of the lake must have left it there for me. Like the kings of old, I have been called on a sacred quest. The magic of humans became mine to grasp" Timothy looked down at his weapon, "It is stronger than rock, yet it is light and well balanced. It can cut through almost anything." Timothy waved the sword about showing how smoothly it glided through the air. Then almost quicker then Toby could register, Timothy sliced a large flower from the honeysuckle plant in which they hid. Timothy moved like an experienced swordsman, graceful and precise. Timothy sheathed his sword gently into the folds of leather in his belt.

"It is only by the magic of my blade that I have survived so long on my own. That and the magic of men that I have attained in my reading."

"Timothy?" Toby asked softly.

"Yes Toby?" Timothy answered, expecting a complex question about his sword.

"What is a book?" Toby asked bluntly.

Timothy paused for a moment and said, "I had a dear friend named Philip who would often say that books are the place men capture their magic and it is the source of all their power."

Timothy stood to his feet and walked to the edge of the honeysuckle bush. "We should get moving. I see no sign of the hawk." As Timothy turned back to see if Toby was in agreement, Toby was chewing on the flower that was cut from the bush.

"These blossoms are amazing!" Toby said with a mouth full of flowers.

"Let us make haste, the morning approaches steady." Timothy said as he lifted the leaves of the plants around them to make an exit.

Toby made his way out as well but only after picking a few more flowers from the bush on his way out. The flowers were bright yellow and white and were almost dripping with nectar. Timothy could recognize the sweet aroma, but did not want to be distracted with simple pleasures. Toby on the other hand, stuck flowers behind his ears to save them for later and then crammed a few more into his mouth as he made his way out onto the path. Timothy turned to make sure Toby was keeping up with him and couldn't help but smile at the sight of him. Toby had what seemed to be a permanent smile on his face and an innocence that Timothy was growing fond of. Something perhaps that Timothy had lost, but being around his new found friend was awakening some of that youthful joy that he once had. As they made their way down the path, the forest was alive with the sounds of insects singing. The level of which had now increased back to normal, helping them to feel at ease as they made their way through the deep forest.

As the two companions make their way through a jagged and cumbersome path. The brush behind them slowly bends and then a quick movement followed by stillness. Unaware that they are being pursued, Timothy and Toby march onward. Timothy keeping a watchful eye ahead as they travel, and Toby asking the occasional convoluted question about quests and ladies in lakes, still trying to wrap his head around Timothy's deeply held beliefs.

The Epic Of Timothy Gray

Chapter Seven
Allies Above

As the two travelers approached a small clearing in the underbrush, they could see early morning clouds glowing warm with morning light through holes in the canopy above. There lay before them a large fallen tree covered in moss and layers of turkey tail mushrooms going up and down the sides of the log. "This seems like the ideal place to forage some breakfast." Timothy's words broke the long silence that they had maintained while furiously navigating through the woods. Toby's face lit up with delight.

The area around them was lush with early blooming red mulberry bushes, edible flowers, mushrooms and even a large hawthorn tree with blooms that were just beginning to show bright red fruit. It had been so long since Timothy had enjoyed such a variety of vegetation in a single location. As Toby began pulling fresh berries from the bushes, Timothy turned over a rock and began munching on grubs. As Timothy chewed on the rather sinewy flesh of a plump caramel colored grub his ears perked up at the soft melody of a song bird in the trees above. The song seemed to shift and change like the radio in the hunting cabin when the humans would tune in to find a song. The volume and flare mesmerized Timothy. Even Toby took notice and stopped stuffing his stained mouth with berries. The sounds became a symphony of birds echoing through the forest, but were very much coming from a single small bird above as it shifted from tree to tree calling out into the woods.

The song bird came down to the fallen tree in the clearing and planted its feet onto the ground, looking directly at Timothy. Although a small bird, she had a beautiful blue beak and layers of deeper and deeper blue going down her back. She puffed up her chest and gave Timothy a long slow gaze as if to see what he was going to do. Timothy pulled the grub from his mouth and spoke up. "You have a lovely song there."

The bird lowered its head to Timothy while tilting to the side as if to measure him up. "You are in danger." she whispered softly.

"Oh, surely not from the likes of you?" Timothy said with a bit of a laugh.

"I saw you fall to the ground. Afraid of a small mad jay. Perhaps you should heed my warning." The bird glanced across the clearing at Toby who was making his way closer to hear the whispering. "Your chubby friend has captured the attention of a hungry fox. He has been following your scent all morning." The bird looked back at Timothy, "I saw what you did for the blue jay's egg. Although futile, it was a kindness that I wish to return."

"Futile?" Timothy questioned.

"Yes, the egg was rotten. But listen now. Your situation is dire. The fox is not far from your trail. You must act now if you wish to survive." The noble bird stated confidently.

"The egg was rotten?" Timothy said, feeling quite disappointed and remembering the pain of falling from the tree.

"Listen carefully, small rodent, you will not survive a confrontation with a fox. Your only hope is to split up from here. For the fox will find his meal." The bird said as she lifted her gaze up to Toby who recoiled in fear. Timothy turned to Toby who looked as if he was about to cry and then back to the bird to respond. "We will not be splitting up. Whatever our fate, we will face it together."

The bird shook its head. "This is the second time I have come to your aid, and it shall be the last. Your shiny stick will not spare you from the cunning fox."

"Second time?" Timothy took a pause.

The bird puffed up its chest again and then let out a loud cry that sent shivers down their spines. "kee-eeeee-arr", It was the distinct sound of a hawk and even though they could tell it was coming from the small bird, they instinctively cowered and looked to the sky. The bird grinned and then took off to the air. "Good luck, rodents." she called out as she flew away.

"Timothy, I can not. I feel scared Timothy, and this feeling scares me. If I face the fox, I will surely die." Toby began rambling.

Timothy, still perplexed as to how they had been fooled before by the clever songs of the mockingbird, began to ponder on their current situation.

"Timothy, you should go. I can't even run, I feel my life slipping from me as I speak." Toby continued on.

"Listen Toby, pull yourself together." Timothy said boldly, "There is a hungry fox pursuing us, yes."

"And it is also true that my skill in battle will be no match for a predator such as this." Timothy spoke as if thinking aloud, unsure of the solution. "But look where we are Toby. Look at the bounty of this clearing. Surely even a fox would give up its pursuit if its hunger was satiated." Timothy's eyes lit up as he reached a moment of epiphany.

"Quick, Toby, we must gather an offering of food. Ripe berries and fruit. Plump grubs and foraged treats. We must pile them up here in the opening. Quickly, we haven't time to waste." Timothy said as he gathered some of his findings and a large leaf from the ground. He placed the leaf out in the opening and tossed his findings onto it. Slowly Toby began to come around and take action. They moved as quickly as they could, tossing fruits and berries into a pile. Within a few minutes they had created a pile taller than Timothy. Timothy split some of the berries and using his blade carved slices of the aromatic hawthorn berries and placed them around the pile while Toby took up shelter inside the decaying log in the center of the clearing. "Timothy" he whispered, "that is more than a fox can eat, let us seek shelter."

Timothy crawled into the log, followed by Toby, deep into the shadows. Through the opening they could just see the distant pile of vegetation. Timothy leaned to one side of the log in quiet anticipation while Toby's nerves had him twisted in small convulsions. "Toby, this will work." Timothy said to encourage his nervous friend.

"I do hope so, but the very thought of facing a creature like this..." Toby trailed off, "Timothy, my family was attacked by coyotes. I only remember the sight of paws pulling dirt away from the opening of our hovel. I was overcome with fear. I felt my life slip away from me. When I awoke again, I was injured and my family was all gone. It is not the teeth nor the claw that terrify me Timothy. I am afraid I will slip away again. I am afraid of being so afraid." Toby began to weep as he shook ever so slightly. His tail curled under him as he faced away from the opening to their hollow shelter. Timothy, unsure of what to say muttered again, "This will work."

A brief time passed before they could hear the faint sound of sniffing around the log. Then Timothy saw it out of the opening. A dull gray fox walked past the entrance and approached the pile of food. The fox sniffed around the pile and then stepped back for a moment of silent introspection over this abundant offering in the clearing. Timothy held his breath. The fox sniffed the pile again and took a single bite. Timothy exhaled a deep breath as his shoulders sank in relief. "It is working." he whispered to Toby, who was too afraid to look, let alone respond.

Suddenly the fox called out, "Is this for me?"

"I know where you hide there in the log. It was very kind of you to leave me such a treat."

Timothy was silent, but his smile grew and he began to radiate pride.

"It doesn't change the fact that I'm going to kill you, but it is ever so thoughtful." The fox continued as Timothy's smile deflated into a look of terror and disappointment.

ad"This is great and all, but I have a female and 4 hungry cubs back in the den. I can not return to them with a few berries. No. Cubs need fat." The fox continued as he began circling the log. "Cubs need flesh." They could now hear footsteps across the top of the log. "Cubs need blood."
The fox yelled loudly before pouncing on the log. The log cracked and dust fell from the top of it onto the two inside. Toby cried out, "No please no." As the fox reared back and pounced again. This time it cracked harder. Timothy reached out for Toby and tugged on him, "We must flee." Timothy spoke but Toby did not respond. His body had gone limp. The fox pounced again, this time his paws bursting through the log, sending debris onto Toby who still did not move. The fox looked through the hole he had created, "There you are." he exclaimed.

Timothy could not pull Toby with him and had to release his friend. He rushed to the opening of the hollow log when suddenly he was tripped by another great thud. And then another. He quickly jumped to the top of the opening and flipped around to face the fox, who was standing over an open hole in the log, but he was looking directly in Timothy's direction.

Timothy drew his sword, "Get away from my friend!" He screamed while clutching his sword with two hands. The fox seemed to be frozen with his front paws buried inside the log. Suddenly Timothy felt the log shake again, but this time he

could tell that the fox was holding very still and not the cause
of this mild tremor. He paused for a brief moment to allow
his mind to catch up to his heart and looked deep into the
foxes eyes and was surprised by what he saw. Fear.

The fox quickly hopped away from the log and then ran
away as fast as any woodland creature had ever seen.
Timothy stood there puzzled, sword in hand, for a moment
wondering if he had possibly frightened the fox with his
blade and heroic poise. For a very brief moment his heart
felt proud and a very dumb grin spilled out onto his face.
Suddenly a shadow loomed over him. Timothy could feel a
warm wind blowing across the tips of his ears. His boost in
self confidence took a very quick dive. Suddenly the wind
reversed and Timothy's ears were pulled up into the air.
As he turned his body slowly his entire field of view was
overcome with the gigantic face of a black bear sniffing
Timothy. Timothy froze in fear. The bear lifted his head a
bit higher and inhaled deeply again. The bear scrunched his
face, unpleased with the aroma. Timothy, frozen in fear, also
noticed a particular stench in the air sniffing himself out of
curiosity. There was a foul stench of rotten flesh. The bear's
attention was turned to the pile of fruits and grubs laid out
on the floor.

The bear sniffed around for a moment and then took a
giant bite. Saliva dripping onto the pile he chewed it as he
continued stuffing more into his jaws. Before long he had
devoured it completely, including the leaves it laid upon.
Timothy was still frozen, but not only because of a fear

of drawing the bear's attention, but also because he was mesmerized by the haste with which the bear consumed the feast. The bear sat down just across from Timothy.

"Was it you small mouse? Who prepared this feast for me?" The bear speculated.

"Why, yes, Yes I did. Did you enjoy the gift?" Timothy played along, unsure if he could make a run for it, and still aware of his friend unconscious in the log below. Afraid to provoke action, Timothy decided to mimic the bear's actions and take a seat as well.

The bear stretched his paws forward. All his claws spread wide and extended. Some of them were as long as Timothy himself. The bear let out a long loud yawn. Timothy was shook by the noise. The deep tones of the bear's yawn made the log beneath him reverberate and Timothy could feel the vibrations in his chest. Never has a mouse come so close to a beast of this size. Timothy tried his best to act calm, pretending as if he normally spoke to bears, hoping the bear would also believe this to be normal.

"Aaaaahhhh yes, I was truly famished. I haven't had a bite to eat in many moons. And just as I awake, I come to find you here with this offering of kindness." The bear seemed to be speaking his thoughts as they occurred to him. His face and eyes followed along with a puzzled look.

"Who are you, small mouse, to pay me such an honor as

this?" The bear leaned in as he spoke.

Timothy began muttering but then spoke up, "Sir, I'm uhm... I am Timothy Gray sir."

"Timothy Gray." The bear responded slowly," And what is it you want of me that you beckon me with the sweet aroma of my favorite fruits?"

Timothy was lost as to what to say, still adlibbing his way through this situation. "Just your friendship sir. That is all."

"You, wish to be friends." The bear sat back in shock. "Why ever would a bear and a mouse be friends?"

Timothy pondered deeply on the profound question. He looked back at the log on which he stood and thought of his friend inside. He looked back up at the bear and spoke boldly, "I too was skeptical of such ideas. But life offers us some challenges that are best not faced alone. And one cannot judge the value of friendship from appearances. If I know anything, it is that courage is not measured in inches, and the weight lifted by friendship is not from a strength found in physical might." Thinking of Toby and their brief time together, Timothy was overtaken by an unfamiliar sense of belonging he had not felt since he was a young mouse in the loving nest of his family. His memories mixed with the recent events and concern for his friend who now laid oddly silent. Timothy's eyes welled up.

The bear's shoulders began to droop as he became relaxed and his apprehensions began to fade as he could sense Timothy's sincerity.

"Alright mouse, If it means that much to you, I will be your friend." The bear responded, attempting to cheer up the small mouse. The bear took his claw and poked a grub that was escaping the pile of treats and reached out to Timothy. The bear's claw was about half the size of Timothy himself. And although deep down Timothy was afraid, he reached out his hands and lifted the skewered grub from the claw of the bear.

"See, we are now friends right?" The bear said optimistically but in a way revealing his lack of familiarity with the concept of friendship.

Timothy nodded and took a bite. The bear continued to gorge himself on the fruits upon the ground. Within a few minutes the bear had consumed everything in sight and was licking his paws. The bear lifted himself slowly from the ground. Timothy who had only nibbled on his grub, sat it down and stood to his feet as well.

"Friend, I do appreciate the feast." The bear said while wiping debris from his chin. "I have never had such a treat upon awakening from my slumber. Nor have I had such a friend as you."

"It was an honor to serve you, friend, what shall I call you?" Timothy responded.

"My mother called me Jeremiah, but she calls me JereBear." the bear said with a smile as he looked just beyond Timothy and then turned to walk away.

Timothy turned to see the mocking bird sitting on a distant limb. She fluttered down to the log and landed next to Timothy.

The bear turned as he walked away, "You never make me a feast Philis. I feel like our new friend has raised the bar."

The mocking bird picked up and yelled loudly, "You know our arrangement JereBear, I pick off the bugs and I get to eat the bugs. I have yet to understand what you get out of this relationship."

The bear laughed and walked off into the woods, "Take care small friends, but I must keep moving to keep things moving, if you know what I mean." As the bear shuffled into the distance. The mocking jay turned to Timothy and let out a giggle. "He is off to drop his first spring droppings." she said as her face turned a more somber tone, "It will not be a pretty sight."

Timothy, quite confused by the entire experience, brought

his attention back to Toby who lay in the log. He rushed
below to grab ahold of him. The smell inside the log was
that of rot and decay. It was nearly unbearable and Timothy
coughed as he dragged his friend out into the daylight.
Toby's body was limp. The mocking jay took notice of the
smell and covered her beak with her wings. "What is that
smell?" she blurted out. Timothy looked at Toby's tail
and saw a green stain on his tail and bottom. Suddenly
Timothy was reminded of Toby's full name and the gander's
comments about the irony of a opossum with the last name
of Greenbottom.

Timothy lifted Toby's eyelid and looked deeply into his eye.
"Are you in there, friend?"

"Did he die?" The mocking bird whispered.

"He has no wounds. And I can feel the life inside of him"
Timothy responded with his hand on Toby's chest. "I believe
this has happened to him before. He seemed to think that his
fear could kill him."

"This smell is going to attract attention. We should not
stay out in the open like this." The mockingbird said, still
covering her beak.

"He is more than I can carry, but I will not leave his side."
Timothy laid, leaning against Toby.

"You are a strange mouse indeed. You stand beside your

friend, no matter the danger... no matter the smell." The mocking bird spoke from behind her wings.

Timothy smiled. "His name is Toby Greenbottom and do not judge him for his current state, for his heart is strong. I am Timothy Gray, pleased to make your acquaintance my lady."

"My lady?... A strange mouse indeed." The mockingbird became embarrassed and hopped up onto the log. "My name is Philis, but you can keep calling me 'my lady'."

"I will keep an eye out for you mouse." Phillis said as she shook her feathers into a fluff. "I do hope to see you again. You and your smelly friend."

With that, she flew off into the treetops. Timothy lay with Toby, still unmoving and quiet in the clearing of the woods. Exhausted from his journey he nuzzled into Toby's side and rested as he looked out into the thick woods unsure about his ability to continue on this journey. His eyes heavy, his energy spent, Timothy slowly closed his eyes.

Chapter Eight
In Pursuit of Answers

Timothy awoke to find his world rocking side to side as he lay straddle across Toby's back. The evening light settled across the forest floor. The air was thick and the clouds rested low on the tree branches leaving limited visibility. Timothy could hear the floor below smoosh under Toby's feet and when he looked down he could see that Toby's feet were sinking into the thick moist ground. Timothy sat up to try and look around. The foliage had changed. They had left the dense woods of the forest and were now pressing through reeds of tall grass in a wet flat land. It was approaching evening in that golden hour when the earth seemed to be painted by a different artist. The sound of Toby's feet squishing into the mud was broken up by the sound of Toby's voice. "Are you awake back there?" Toby came to a stop.

The Epic Of Timothy Gray

Timothy hopped off Toby and slid down a nearby blade of grass. "Toby, are you alright? I was afraid I had lost you there."

Toby looked down ashamed, "Oh, I'm sorry for that, I was overtaken with fear. It is something that I cannot control. I awoke and you were right there by my side." Toby looked up with a smile.

"And you carried me through the day I see." Timothy, still a little groggy, looked around to get his bearings.

"It was the least I could do Timothy. You fought off a fox for me!" Toby exclaimed.

Timothy's eyes widened, not sure how to explain the events of the morning. He opened his mouth to speak, but before he could a voice from above chirped down to them.

"I may have been a little fuzzy with the details." Said the mockingbird, rested upon a tall cat tail reed. "But to be fair, the story of the mouse who fought off the fox made for great gossip across the forest breeze. Those cardinals love a good story."

Timothy smiled, "but the truth is Toby..." Timothy took pause while seeing the admiration in Toby's eyes. "...the truth is that it was a team effort." Toby smiled large.

"Our bird friend, my lady, directed me through the forest."

Timothy looked up at Phillis, the mocking jay, "I may have also told him to call me that." she sputtered. Then she looked embarrassed and fluttered to a lower position.

"Your smelly friend tells me that you were looking for owls. I'm not sure why a mouse would be chasing owls, but I am afraid you are out of luck. The owls that normally hunt the forest have been a rare sight this season."

Timothy looked down, his feet sinking into the wet ground as his spirit also sank. "I had been told that the homeland of the owls was just beyond the forest. Perhaps this has all been for nothing."

Phillis hopped closer and stretched her wing out to comfort Timothy. "I am sure we can find the owls you seek dear." she gave Timothy a shake, "and then they can gobble you right up."

"They might try, but Timothy is an owl hunter.", spouted Toby. Phillis glanced down to see Timothy's sword dangling from his belt. She slightly recoiled as Timothy pulled his feet from the mud and continued onward.

"If you really want to find someone in the forest, perhaps you should speak to the soul of the forest.", Philis said.

The Epic Of Timothy Gray

"Who is this soul of the forest?" Toby blurted out.

"The Loski, also called the soul of the forest, is the keeper of knowledge for the lowland forests. A century old box turtle. Generations have come to him to share their stories and all winged creatures whisper the breeze of the forest to him. If anyone in all the land knows where the owls currently reside, the Loski will know.", Phillis explained with excitement.

Timothy perked up, "Then we must go see this Loski. Where might we find him?"

"The Loski is not far, but tradition and honor require that we must provide a gift. Do you have anything to offer as a gift?"

"I have but my sword and cloak, and these I can not give. What does such an aged box turtle desire as tribute?" Timothy queried.

Phillis explained further, "Loski is so old, they say he never leaves his burrow. He survives on the offerings brought to him by visitors who seek knowledge or have a story to tell."

Toby pulled his hand out of the tmud with squishy slurping noise. "How about one of these?" Toby asked as he lifted his hand to reveal a long squirming earthworm wrapped between his fingers and around his hand. "I keep finding them under the mud, and they are quite tasty." Toby continued.

Phillis' eyes widened, "Oh, those are a treat indeed."

Timothy scrunched his nose in mild disgust. "Perhaps we should gather a few on our journey to the turtle, and if nothing better presents itself..." Timothy let a shiver run down his spine, "We can offer him the worms."

Timothy found the sight of worms unappealing. It reminded him of the horrors of his youth, seeing his mother opened up by the talon of an owl.

Toby clawed the muddy ground in front of him exposing a deeper layer of moist earth with holes beneath where worms and critters burrowed.

"I have found lots of them and I can find more!" Toby said ecstatically, excited to be able to offer his special talents to the group. Timothy wrapped a leaf from a nearby vine into a makeshift basket and taking the earthworm from Toby's hand, he placed it inside, being sure to express his disgust as he did.

"If you follow the shoreline from here, you will arrive at Loski's burrow by morning. Just be sure not to get into the deep silt and soft mud. Sometimes creatures get stuck, especially heavier creatures." She looked up accusingly at

Toby, whose hands were buried in the mud up to his wrists.

"Thank you my lady" Timothy bowed, "we are again in your debt."

Phillis covered up her giggling grin in embarrassment. "Oh Timothy Gray, you are a different mouse. You know I have heard your name being whispered in the breeze. They say you possess human magic. I am not quite sure if I believe that, but you are quite unique." Philis looked at the basket folded from a leaf holding the worm, "You do seem to have mastered some human skills."

"I do like the way he talks." Toby blurted in.

"I have learned much from the humans and their magic. This was a spell I learned from a book on basket weaving." Timothy said proudly, "Humans have many books on all forms of skill and magic."

"Humans keep their magic in books you say?" Philis pried, looking for something juicy to share with her winged friends.

"Well, sort of. The real magic, or so I have discovered, is not in the words in the books, it is in the belief that those words can be true." Timothy explained.

Toby and Philis gave a puzzled look, not quite understanding.

"I have witnessed a human pick up a small book, read its words and then use those spells to build something that before was not there, but then came into being through their faith in the words they read."

"Reading is a powerful tool, but believing, believing is where magic manifests." Timothy spoke, remembering his old friend Philip who taught him first to read, but never quite had the faith to believe what he read. For Philip only read to entertain his mind. Timothy has learned from watching the humans interact with books that there was more to this human magic than mere spells on paper.

Toby interrupted Timothy, "found another one!" As he pulled a long plump worm from the ground and laid it in the basket.

"I would like to hear more about this one day, Timothy Gray, but I do have a nest of my own to care for.", Philis reached into the basket and took the largest worm.

Phillis hopped to a higher position on a reed and announced, "I do hope to run into you two again. Good luck on your journey." Muffled by the large worm in her beak. And with that, Phillis leaped to the air and fluttered away.

Timothy and Toby looked at each other and shrugged. "I guess we owe her one." Timothy said with a deep breath. They drudged through the mire, being cautious to avoid wet areas and taking their time to collect a few more earthworms along the way. Toby was sure to sample every third worm, as he said to "ensure their quality."

Chapter Nine
Seeking Wisdom

The air above grew thick with fog and the leaves and grasses were moist with beads of water droplets accumulating on their surface. As Timothy Gray and Tobias Greenbottom entered into a gentle brook covered with small smooth pebbles the thick foliage opened up to a crowded community of woodland creatures. Most seemed to be standing in line, queuing up to a steep bank of rock and clay soil, covered with moss and winding vines. Two towering blue herons stood on either side of a wide opening in the riverbank, their legs shooting up from the mud like pillars. The crowd of critters composed of mice, rats, a couple squirrels, and an armadillo were all quietly waiting in front of the mouth of the opening in the riverbank. There was a silent reverence among the crowd and faint whispers coming from front, just beyond view.

The Epic Of Timothy Gray

Toby cleaned his hands in the clear running waters that just barely covered the pebbled surface, "Are we there yet Timothy?" Toby burst out loud, breaking the reverent silence. Those near the back of the line looked back to see Toby and Timothy entering the brook .

Timothy whispered, "I believe perhaps we have...", Timothy gulped as the crowd made brief eye contact and then began to turn back, "...arrived." he said even more softly. Timothy slowly approached the wide bodied armadillo that seemed to be holding the position at the end of the line. Thinking it wise to confirm with someone about the location of this fabled Loski, Timothy reached up to tap the armadillo on the back. Timothy noticed the armadillo's back and paused himself from touching. The armadillo was covered in scars and scratches on his thick leathery hide. The closer one looked the more one would see that this armadillo's armor tells a long story of warfare and violence. Claw marks and bite marks. If this plated armor could show you its history one would likely avert their gaze just as Timothy began to do as he steadied his nerves and tapped the armadillo on the back.

"Excuse me sir, but we are wondering if we have come to the right place." Timothy spoke softly, "we are seeking the wisdom of the Loski."

The armadillo turned slowly revealing his long haired underbelly. In his hand a staff made of hickory wood encompassed with decorative engravings. He looked at the pair, eyeing their basket of earthworms that was overflowing with wriggling worms.

"What be right for you, mouse? I cannot say, but Loski does reside here." the armadillo said with a gravelly voice. He stared directly at the basket of worms as he continued on, "two types, those who seek Loski, those with a story to tell, and those with a question, and I see that you are the latter."

Timothy looked down at the basket of worms and then up at the mysterious armadillo. "How can you tell?"

"You carry a prize to barter for a story," he responded.

Timothy looked around to see if the Armadillo was carrying anything other than his staff, "And you sir, what prize do you bring?"

"I bring only my story, so that it may be known for all ages," the armadillo retorted, "Loski loves many treats, but none more than a true tale such as what I bring. A story of honor and strife, politics and war, diplomacy, peace, and above all, loyalty," he spoke as his eyes wandered off into the skies above as if he was following his memories as they were carried off into the breeze.

Toby interjected abruptly, "These worms are very fresh and oh so tender-delicious!" Toby licked his lips with a proud grin on his face. The armadillo looked down to the basket in Timothy's hands as the worms squirmed in a balled knot of worm flesh. "You know, it might be best if I let you pass ahead of me. Loski can enjoy your worms while I recount the saga of the counsel of the forest and my time spent in faithful service." the old armadillo again began to float off in words and thought. It was becoming obvious to Timothy that this armadillo was indeed quite old and beyond the worn armor, he had old eyes and a sickly complexion. His staff looked as though it was a warrior's weapon but was being utilized as a cane for a doddering elder.

"If you think it best, we will do as you ask, but only if you insist." Timothy responded.

"Oh I do, please." the armadillo stretched out his hand, gesturing to them to pass into the space ahead of him. As they moved toward the entrance they could hear the faint words being discussed ahead of them and they could see Loski, who, for all the hype and lore, was a small box turtle, not even as large as Toby. His skin wrinkled and dry in complex folds. His eyes seemed attentive but barely opened as he looked down over his nose at the small assembly of squirrels before him. His shell seemed perfectly round with bits of mud and moss at the edges. He was laying on a rock just slightly elevated above where the two squirrels stood below sharing what sounded like a disagreement over property rights to burial grounds. It appeared that Loski was being asked to judge in the matter. Loski would pause, sometimes close his eyes as if to capture a quick nap or contemplate his thoughts and then respond. His voice was a strong whisper, soft but confident. Timothy leaned in to hear him give his ruling to the squirrels.

"When you bury your nuts, it matter not where, because they do not all belong to you. For every nut you bury for yourself, also bury one for the tree that provided it, and one for the squirrel that planted that tree before you were ever born. In this way, there will be nuts for you, nuts for your neighbor, and a tree for your future offspring." Loski spoke in a long winded breath with short breaks to inhale. "If you all do so, there will be no need to quarrel over whose territory is whose. For the land belongs to none of us, but we are merely borrowing from it and we will return to it."

The squirrels seemed inspired by the words and after leaving a pile of seeds and small berries in front of their host, they scampered off together.

The line moved forward and continued like this for a while. Animals seeking wisdom, some even just asking for a blessing, treating the turtle as some form of spiritual leader. All the while, the large blue herons stood above, although not looking down, they seemed to be listening in on every conversation. Just in front of Toby and Timothy was a lone female field mouse carrying many small pouches and bags of brightly colored mushrooms.

When it came time for the lady mouse to be heard, she laid her bags down gently before Loski and stepped forward and spoke timidly "I have done as you asked when I came to you last. I collected for you these exotic growths from the forest floor."

The turtle's eyes grew wide. "Oh you have done well. And as I have promised, the solution to your problem." The Loski turned his eyes to a small rabbit who quickly hopped back into the opening behind the turtle and just as soon returned with a small bulbous sack and placed it in front of the young lady mouse.

"Take these dry peppers and carefully place them on the tops of your blackberry bush. This will discourage the deer from devouring your home's cover and all the fruit that nourishes your family in the long summer months."

The young lady mouse picked up the small pouch and hoisted it over her shoulder.

"Be cautious and keep it closed until you are ready to use it." The turtle warned, "You do not want to crack those dried peppers open nor do you want to let them touch you as that could be the worst day of your life."

"Thank you great Loski", whispered the mouse as she bowed down. "blessings to you child., do tell your mother I said hello." The Loski said with a grin, looking down at the mushrooms which the rabbit now dragged back into the hovel behind him.

The lady mouse walked by as Toby and Timothy stepped

forward and their eyes met briefly. The mouse, having looked at Timothy's strange attire, let out a little giggle as she passed by. Timothy, having not seen any of his kind in a long while, stared awkwardly with a goofy grin. His attention turned as they stepped forward before the ancient turtle. Looking up at the tall birds on either side, towering over them. They came forward in reverence and laid their offering of worms overflowing from the basket before the Loski.

The Loski looked down at the offering, wiggling and writhing and then looked back up at the two companions who kept their heads bowed, unsure how to begin this exchange.

The Loski took a deep breath, "Timothy Gray!"

Timothy looked up in surprise.

"I have heard all about you." The crowd around all froze at the mention of his name, all eyes now on Timothy as the sage old turtle continued. "Oh how I have been looking forward to our visit."

The Epic Of Timothy Gray

Chapter Ten
A Fork in the Path

All the creatures coming and going had now turned and drawn themselves in close to the hovel of the soul of the forest. They all listened attentively, for they had all heard the whispers on the breeze. They had heard the name of this small mouse from the prairie and his companion. The gander had surely done as he had promised. But what had they heard? What stories were shared and how much had they been exaggerated. Timothy was full of anxiety when he responded, "You know my name?"

"Oh I'm afraid the whole of the forest now knows your name Timothy Gray. The forest breeze is layered with songs singing your praises. A hero of the common beast, so they say. Some claim you harness the magic of humans." The turtle said, giving Timothy a sideways glare. "Is this true? Do you practice the sorcery of man?"

Timothy looked around at the many who surrounded him with an uneasy stare. "I have read the knowledge of man. I have learned to harness tools and become more than a meager mouse. This is true."

"Is there more to being what we were created to be? Don't be fooled by the magic of man, my young rodent friend. There is no higher calling than for one to become what we were created to be. To achieve anything different is not higher or lower in stature, it is simply a lie. One that I see you have come to believe." the turtle said while looking down to Timothy's sword hanging from his belt.

"I believe that I am called to a greater purpose than to cower and hide as a mouse. I have been chosen by the gods to make a stand against the tyranny of nature. This I do believe." Timothy stated bravely.

"A lie believed is more powerful than a truth denied. You are proof of that my friend. Just be warned, human magic will lead you down a path of destruction from which you can not return." The Loski spoke, lifting his head up higher, "I understand it is vengeance you seek."

"I wish to avenge my family, yes. I seek justice." Timothy answered.

"Justice... Vengeance... these are human desires. Dark magic indeed." The turtle said, lowering his head.

"And what of honor... loyalty... courage. Are these not also human sorcery?" Timothy rebutted.

"You are not the first to come to me with these spells, young rodent." The turtle said with a quick glance toward the armadillo who seemed to have an expression of admiration and gave Timothy a knowing look and a subtle nod. "As for the gods... there is one true creator, and he had the wisdom to make you a mouse. The sooner you come to accept that truth, the less your suffering will be."

Timothy, worried that he wasn't getting out of this conversation what he came for, tried to change the subject. "Tell me of the days of thunder, the day my family was slaughtered in the mighty oak tree."

"Oh, hmmm." The turtle pondered, as if the question inspired a thought. "Yes... maybe you should see the great heights and tragic depths of human magic. The days of thunder, the day the earth was split open and the great barrier was placed by the humans. You must travel to the great barrier and see for yourself. Follow the setting sun for a few more days until you reach the great barrier. Once you have come to see the pinnacle of human magic, if you wish to continue on this path set before you, you only need to cross the barrier into the deep forest on the other side.

The Epic Of Timothy Gray

There you will find the long horned owls breeding ground. If any remain. For you see, the days of thunder were not just a slaughter of your kin, but of the entire forest. And since those days the slaughter has continued as the great barrier has cut through the land and destroyed the patterns of the forest that had previously survived many moons before you and I and our ancestors before us." The turtle paused sorrowfully.

The animals around all looked down to the ground and a sense of sadness swept through those present. Timothy Gray was puzzled but could recognize grief when he saw it. And that was the look on the crowd, as though everyone had lost someone to this great barrier.

"Young Timothy," The turtle broke the silence. "There will come a time when you have travelled too far down this path of human vengeance. You must choose to turn around and accept your created being before it is lost and corrupted by this human magic." the turtle said softly and compassionately as if he was fighting for Timothy's very soul.

Timothy respectfully responded, "I will heed your words wize Loski. I will seek the barrier, but I fear that I know no other path than the one I am on. I must see this to its end, even if it is also mine."

Toby, worried his opportunity would pass, spoke up. "I had a question too if you don't mind."

The turtle turned his attention to Toby who stepped forward

from behind Timothy and spoke up. "When I am afraid, I lose myself. I am overcome with fear and I die. At least it feels like dying…" Toby looked around and realized that he had everyone's attention now too and it made him nervous. "How can I not be afraid any more?"

"Fear is often the natural response to danger. And one cannot overcome nature, despite what your friend here may think." The Loski said turning back to Timothy, "but young rodent friend, maybe you can tell your companion. How does one respond to fear?" There was a brief moment of silence as the turtle looked deep into Timothy's eyes. Timothy thought and then looked over toward his warm hearted friend. "Courage… the proper response to fear is courage. I too am afraid, Toby. But I can not let fear win the day, so I call upon courage to overcome fear." Timothy's voice shook with a vulnerable honesty.

"I think your friend speaks truth to you Toby, for although he is a deeply confused mouse, his magic has a lot to be admired. But you Toby, also have nothing to be ashamed of. Not everyone can wield a sword and battle large predators. You have a sacred job to do. Make sure your friend here takes the right path. For he may save your skin, but you may save his soul."

The Loski looked down as the worms had begun to work their way out of the basket attempting to escape and find their way back into the earth. "I must speak now with an old friend over these delicious treats. Please send word and let me know how your journey ends." With that the turtle bit into an escaping worm and choked it down inch by inch. The armadillo walked up and greeted the turtle, "old friend, you always have the right words" They greeted each other by pressing their heads against the other as if they were close friends. "Now where did I leave off when we last spoke?" The two continued on as the armadillo shared stories of forest politics. Toby and Timothy stepped back and before they could hear much more they were confronted by the small lady mouse from before.

"I understand you are heading to the barrier and beyond?" She said carefully toting the bag she was given. "You will need a guide, the barrier is a death trap to those who go unprepared. I am from the land across the barrier, I am going there now. Perhaps I could guide you if you agree, and perhaps in exchange... you could help me transport my cargo?" She asked looking down at the sack in her hands.

Timothy tried to respond but tripped on his words, "that is, well would be, if I may, that sounds..."

"Splendid!" Toby interjected, "That would be ever so lovely. Never had a guide before, but this is my first grand adventure. Allow me." Toby took the bag with this tail curled around it and rested it on his back. He turned to Timothy who still seemed frozen in thought and said "we have a guide now, what a trio we have become."

Timothy snapped out of it, "splendid, splendid indeed. Yes,

very lovely." He said as he made eye contact with the lady mouse. Suddenly he felt a type of fear he had never had to face before, he felt embarrassed, fearful of making a bad impression. This was an unsettling fear that Timothy had no experience with. Being alone most of his life Timothy had had many encounters with other rodents and a wide variety of forest animals, but somehow contact with other field mice had evaded him. And this field mouse in particular had a delicate demeanor and soft voice that struck a chord in Timothy's inner being that he had never felt before.

Timothy looked away quickly feeling he was failing horribly at making a good impression. "Toby, what say we let the lady ride with the cargo, at least until we get onto dry ground."

"My lady?" Toby said, feeling magnanimous, he lowered his shoulder and head to the ground for her to climb aboard. "Honestly, I would normally not accept, but dragging those mushrooms all this way has left me a little feeble. Thank you. And my name is Lydia by the way."

Timothy perked up, realizing he hadn't been clear minded enough for a proper introduction. "I am..."

"Timothy Gray", she interrupted, "yes I was there."

She let out a giggle. "And you must be Tobias, his faithful companion. I have heard the whispers of the forest wind. Stories of your adventures have spread quickly. I am glad to make your acquaintance."

She climbed on to Toby's back. "Well, the sun is near the horizon, let us make haste." Timothy spoke up with some authority and took off leading the way with Toby and Lydia lagging behind him. He liked to think that he was leading the way to protect their path, but if he was honest with himself, he was avoiding eye contact.

Chapter Eleven
Anything Is Possible

The trio followed the sunset well into the late evening until it grew dark. Toby kept Lydia entertained with stories of their adventures, including how Timothy single handedly defeated a fox and saved Toby's life. Timothy remained focused on navigating through the woods in the dark. He would stop occasionally and look into the night sky, waiting for clouds to pass so he could see the stars. He had picked up a small stick along the hike and would use it to draw an imaginary line through the sky and point in a direction. Lydia watched inquisitively and after a few times of doing this she asked, "the sun has set long ago. Normally I would stop for the night to avoid getting lost. How is it you know where we are going?"

Timothy paused and collected his thoughts, "well, the

humans call it astronomy. They read the stars in the sky to guide their way. I used to look into the sky and see chaos, too many stars to count, but now I see a lion, a big bear and a smaller bear, and a little later this evening the mighty Hercules will appear in the Eastern sky. But most important of all is that star right there." Timothy stretched his stick up to point into the sky. "That is the northern star, and it always stays in the same position in the sky, allowing me to navigate so long as the sky is clear enough to find it."

Lydia moved her head close to Timothy to line up the stick to the star he was pointing out. He could feel her brushing up against him and it tickled his whiskers, making him feel both comfort and fearful all at once.

"So this is human magic?" She whispered in his ear. "Fascinating." Her soft spoken words sent a shiver down his spine.

"One of many human books I have read full of spells like these which give one mastery of this world." Timothy said with admiration. "I have read books on topics from survival, hunting large animals, trapping, fishing, medicinal plants, and many, many books on human history." Timothy paused feeling as though he might be showing off a little too much, fearful he would embarrass himself.

Lydia leaned over and placed her hand on his shoulder and said "you are a very special mouse Timothy Gray." As she let her hand fall from his shoulder stroking his arm Timothy felt a sensation that he hadn't felt since he was a small mouse in his mothers arms. Timothy knew he was unique among all the wildlife of the forest. He knew he was very different. More cunning, more savage, more courageous, and more fierce than most any creature he had come across, but it wasn't until Lydia touched his arm and whispered those words that he actually felt special. The closest feeling he could equate it to was when his mother had picked him up in her arms and whispered to him how proud she was of him. Timothy felt as though he was glowing in the dark of night. He felt a warmth so unfamiliar and yet so nourishing to his spirit that a slight grin came to his face.

Suddenly a low rumble came from ahead of them on their path. A growl but deeper than any beast Timothy had heard, shaking the very ground beneath his feet. Everyone froze in place holding their breath. The grass ahead was tall and swaying in the night breeze. As the trio held their breath in silence they could hear a breathing animal just ahead of them whose breath seemed to produce a breeze of its own, shifting the tips of the tall grasses.

Timothy held his hand up to the others and gestured them to step away slowly, and without a word they both understood and obeyed. Timothy though let his curiosity get the better of him. He walked forward to peek through the thick grasses between them and the beast. He continued to gesture to his friends to hold back as he stepped through the grasses toward the source of the breathing.

The Epic Of Timothy Gray

As he delicately stepped into a flattened clearing he beheld
the sight of a massive bison. With patches of thick brown
fur covering its robust frame and an even thicker heavy
dark mane surrounding its ridged face, with two long dark
horns protruding from the sides of its head. Its eyes darker
than the darkest night sky reflected the stars above. The
bison looked down at Timothy as he entered the clearing.
It breathed out a long huff that nearly knocked Timothy
backwards. "Leave me be, mouse."

Timothy leaned forward and spoke up, "Pardon us, we were
just passing through. We mean you no harm."

"None can harm me any longer. I have laid down for the
last time." The bison looks down at its hind legs and his
leg twitches. In the moonlight Timothy can make out fresh
scratches and bite marks. The bison is injured, but nothing
that should immobilize a beast of this size, just surface
injuries.

"These will heal my friend. No need to surrender so quickly."
Timothy tried to encourage the beast.

"Trust me small mouse, I did not give up easily. I am much
older than my kind has ever been, and my body has begun
to betray me in my old age. These wounds are just the latest
shame to be heaped upon me. I have no herd. I have no
purpose. I come lay here to die." The bison spoke somberly.

Timothy stepped forward and sat down with the bison in his wallow. "I know how it feels, my large friend, to lose everything. I too have many times laid down and thought deeply about just letting the earth swallow me up."

"And what drives you to get back up?" The bison enquired.

Timothy thought long and hard for a moment, "possibilities. I believe that when I do nothing, nothing will change. Nothing is possible, but if I rise up and do something, anything at all, then anything becomes possible."

There was a long moment of silence. Toby and Lydia poked their heads through the grasses and slowly walked toward where Timothy sat.

"I am sure one day, I will have no more fight within me. I am sure I will lie down and wait for death to take me. I hope that on that day, a friend comes along and tells me to get up." Timothy said as he looked around at his friends.

The bison huffed and then turned his head and lay down.

Timothy rose to his feet and yelled "GET UP!".

The bison was a little offended to have such a tiny creature bark orders at him. He gave a snarled growl.

Timothy aggressively stepped forward and yelled again, "GET UP!"

The bison lifted its head and huffed again, looking at the small mouse who posed an aggressive and commanding stance. Timothy stepped right up to his nose and spoke firmly again. "Perhaps your kind knows not what it means to be proud and strong." The bison's brow furled and showed overflowing contempt for the small mouse. "GET UP I SAY!" Timothy shouted again.

The bison became angry and huffed while kicking its legs until it had climbed to its feet and hovered high above Timothy and his friends. "Alright mouse, you have made me angry!" The bison barked back at Timothy as it dragged its feet in the dirt ready to charge. "You know what will happen now, small rodent!?"

Timothy looked up at him and spoke softly, "Anything. Anything is possible now."

The bison's anger subsided quickly. All the offence it had taken at having a small mouse tell him what to do became overshadowed by the idea that maybe this small mouse might have a point.

"Who are you?" The bison asked as it lowered its head to be eye to eye with Timothy.

"Sir, I am Timothy Gray, at your service." Timothy said with a bow. "These are my companions, Toby and Lydia."

The bison took a deep breath in and out, his breath still powerful and blowing past the trio with great force. "I appreciate your words of encouragement, Timothy Gray. I am called Ulysses. Unfortunately words do not greatly change my circumstance." The bison raised his head, "I am still feeble and my bones grind against each other causing great pain. I also have a pack of coyotes who pursue me daily. Eventually, I will not be able to fight them off any longer."

"But not today?" Timothy asked.

"No. Not today." The bison chuckled.

"Today is sometimes all we are given, so let us do with it what we can." Timothy said with a smile and then hopped up and continued on his way.

"Where are you going, that you should travel through the night?" The bison asked as they all started to leave him.

"We travel to the great barrier and beyond." Toby piped up, wanting to take part.

"You can cross the great barrier?" The bison perked up with excitement. "We can." Answered Lydia.

The Epic Of Timothy Gray

"Do you wish to join us?" Asked Timothy.

"If I am to die, I would like to die in the land of my father. I have been separated from my herd since before the humans built the great barrier. I would cherish the opportunity to join you." The bison said humbly.

"See friend... anything is possible." Timothy smiled and then turned to lead the way.

Chapter Twelve
An Introduction To Magic

It didn't take long before the bison offered to let them ride upon his back. He did after all, even at his slower pace, walk faster than the rest of the party. He determined, as embarrassing as it is to allow small creatures to ride upon him, at least he wouldn't have to worry about stepping on someone. This allowed for our adventurers to focus on navigation and some much needed rest.

"Will you teach me more human magic Timothy?" Toby burst out while the trio rocked back and forth upon the bison's back nestled into his bushy mane.

Timothy thought for a moment, "I think the most useful bit of human magic is knot tying. There are few circumstances that cannot be made better with a bit of string and a few knots."

Timothy took some strands of the bison's long dark hairs and began weaving them into a braid. "Watch carefully and do as I do." He slowed down and step by step guided them into making a long braid, then he cut the braids off and showed them how to braid more hair into that braid creating a long piece of thin but sturdy string made from bison hair.

As they worked slowly to follow Timothy's example, Toby struggled to maintain the braided pattern and needed extra help. Lydia picked it up quickly and asked Timothy, "Who taught you this human magic?"

Timothy pondered for a moment, "I think it was a human named Ashley. At least that was the name of the book. The Ashley Book of Knots. At the time, I didn't read so well, but there were pictures that represented reality. I later came to understand words written down also represented reality. I believe when humans master reality, they bind that reality into spells in words printed in books, then other humans can study those spells as I have and bring those words back into reality. This is the way of human magic." Timothy explained while finishing a long strand of string.

"Now let's see that satchel" Timothy motioned toward Toby who still balanced the cargo on his back holding it firm with his tail.

Toby handed him the satchel and then Timothy demonstrated how to tie the most basic knot, a square not. He had them practice on their strands and hooked them all together until they had made a long strap for Lydia's precious cargo. At which point Timothy demanded that Toby try it out. With the new strap made of bison hair the cargo now rested right between Toby's shoulder blades, centered on his back.

"Well this is just lovely, and now my tail is free for something else!" Toby glowed with excitement.

"Is all human magic that easy to learn?" Lydia asked.

Timothy thought for a minute, "in a way, yes. Why, I even sewed my own garments and belt with needle and thread, which is not much different than making string and tying knots. One thing builds onto another. I suppose with enough spells and time to study them, one could do anything using human magic."

Timothy looked into the distant horizon. With the sun rising behind them but still low in the sky, he could see the half moon just over the western horizon. "I once read a story about men who traveled all the way to the moon."

Toby sat straight up and looked toward the moon, "Impossible!"

"On the contrary, they seem to have proved it quite possible. They walked upon its surface and returned back to tell the story." Timothy rebutted.

"But Timothy how? How did they get way up there?", Lydia questioned.

"Well I suppose it was a process. It probably involved many steps. There may be a hundred steps before one can get to the moon. And I have no idea what steps two through ninety-nine are, but I do know what step one is." Timothy said joyously.

"And what is that?" Lydia questioned.

Toby was looking up at the moon with a dreamy expression on his face, as if he had had an epiphany and he whispered, "They believed it to be possible."

Timothy smiled wide, "Precisely!", Timothy shouted, he turned to Lydia, "step one is always to believe in what is possible", Timothy leaned over and patted Tobias in the back. "You are beginning to see it now, friend. Belief, that is the source of all human magic."

Toby looked back at his friend smiling, proud to have learned about human magic, but still marveling about how they got all the way to the moon. He thought about how much he would like to be more like Timothy, fearless, brave, and capable of anything. Much like the moon, the distance to where he was and where he wanted to be seemed immeasurably vast.

Lydia wasn't looking at the moon. She was looking at the way Timothy looked at the moon. There was something about him that seemed so exotic and dangerous to her way of life, yet when she looked into his eyes, she saw right past his courageous display and she could see a kindness that was clouded in sorrow. Lydia felt drawn to Timothy, not because of his strength, but because he had a hurt and she had a natural desire to heal.

The bison slowed to a stop, having listened to their conversation, he looked up toward the moon. He hadn't given much consideration to the things he believed. A few days ago, he wouldn't have thought it possible that he would allow small friends to ride upon his back, let alone that he would have small friends. Magic can not be so simple as believing, he thought. Yet, here he is on a journey to cross the barrier, something he very firmly once believed to be impossible, but at this moment was beginning to believe and believing was manifesting into becoming. He stared briefly, wide eyed into the moon, so deep that his black eyes reflected it perfectly as he had this one joyful thought. "Maybe anything is possible." He muttered under his breath to himself.

The bison sniffed the air and caught something afoul. He

turned his head, while rotating to check behind their path. The breeze shifted and was now coming from the east. The bison sniffed again deeply and then held his breath. He looked steadily out in the eastern horizon, back on the path that they had just come from. Everyone on top of the bison held still, unsure of what was going on. Suddenly, the bison clinched up, and everyone was shook. The bison softly, but firmly spoke. "Everyone... hold on tight."

Chapter Thirteen
To The Moon

The three companions grabbed fistfuls of the bison's curly mane, and they darted off so quickly each flew upward into the air and just as quickly slammed back down. The ride up until now had been luxurious by comparison. Nothing could have prepared them for this. They each let out squeaks and grunts as they bounced up and down, losing their grip and then reaching deeper for another handful.

At first, no one had time to process what was going on, then they heard the howling and barking of a hungry pack of coyotes. Timothy looked behind them and beyond the dust cloud that Ulysses was kicking up, he could make out at least three pouncing creatures attempting to encircle them while they ran. Timothy could tell by the shifting sway of their movement that Ulysses was struggling and likely in pain, favoring one hind leg over the other. They ascended up a hill, slowing down even further. The three coyotes could easily be seen now, one on each side while another was closely approaching them at the rear.

Just when they reached the peak of the hill the coyote behind them caught up to the heels of Ulysses. They came to a quick and unexpected stop causing the entire trio to flip end over end and land on Ulysses' head between his horns. The coyotes nipped at his heels and he instinctively bucks his hind legs and hit one of the coyotes right in the side. It yipped and cried. Ulysses looked ahead, the reason he had come to an abrupt stop was the utter lack of path ahead of them. The hill they had climbed had a steep cliff crevasse running across the length of the entire hilltop, like the earth itself had cracked open. They were trapped. The coyotes growling and nipping, Ulysses spinning and kicking unsure of where his enemies were as they bit at his lower extremities. The bison turned again to face the gulf before them. The distance to the other side was a good distance and the other side appeared even higher in elevation. Ulysses squared up with the ledge as if he was thinking about attempting the jump.

To all those riding atop the bison, the idea of jumping that distance increasingly felt like a horrible idea. The fall into the crevasse was deep. The kind of depth that one hopes is deadly. One would hope they wouldn't survive that fall only to bake in the hot sun trapped in an inescapable crack in the earth. Of all of them, it was Timothy who spoke up and said what they were all thinking, "impossible."

Ulysses shifted his weight back onto his hind legs, coyotes still nipping at his rear and he loudly growled "anything is possible!" And from a standing position he flung himself upward and outward over the gorge as he shouted "TO THE MOON!"

Everyone, with the exception of the coyotes, took flight through the air, experiencing what Timothy would later attest to be the exact thing Buzz Aldrin experienced when jumping on the moon. A sensation of weightlessness. All three, drifting through space, tethered to the bison by his coarse mane hair. How do birds not faint with every flap of their wings at the sheer dread of this feeling? Timothy pondered feeling his insides levitate as if they would leave his body entirely. In that moment the bison, the lady mouse, Timothy and even the coyotes had a look of intense fright at what was taking place. But in that brief moment, none could bear witness, but if they could, they would have seen a opossum smiling ear to ear with his tongue flapping out the side of his mouth, eyes wide open fully enjoying the ride.

To everyone's surprise they not only cleared the gorge, but overshot the landing heading down hill on the other side. Down a steep hill. There was no stopping. They were fully committed to a gallop pace, one that Ulysses would normally not be able to maintain with his painful hip. They were all worried. All but Toby, who was still having the time of his life bouncing up and down on top of the bison's head while Timothy and Lydia held on tightly to his horns. They continued down the hill at a falling pace for quite some time. Then came the foliage. To their benefit, the bushes slowed them down a little. Branches could be heard crashing and cracking below them as Ulysses began passing through small trees and brush on his way down, still somehow maintaining his footing. Finally they came out into a clearing, having slowed down quite a bit and the ground leveling off just enough to come to a stop. By this time, Toby was hanging on to the tail of the bison. Timothy dangling from his ear and Lydia buried face first deep into his mane atop his head. Ulysses had sticks and leaves poking out his fur in every direction.

The coyotes could be heard howling in the distance. They were smart enough to not attempt a jump of that magnitude. Especially after watching the less than graceful landing on the other side. They had traveled out of view of the coyotes and their free fall escape had probably bought them some time. As they each caught their breath, they began to appreciate the view from where they were.

There before them was a wide and turbulent river with long sandy banks. The river was dark red and looked thick and soft like a satin blanket, but it seemed to swirl and swell as if great river monsters wrestled beneath the surface. The bison spoke up, "tread carefully, small friends, the sandy banks of this river are like a human trap, it will pull you down and not let go."

Toby heard the distant howl of coyotes and asked "is there a way to cross?"

"I crossed it once and I barely survived. We can attempt it, but we must find a rocky path, or we can part ways and you can attempt to swim. I would prefer if my final resting place was not in that cursed silt."

"We should stick together", Timothy exclaimed, "Lydia, how do you get across?"

"Well, I sometimes take the human path." Lydia answered.

"Can you guide us to it?" Timothy pleaded.

Lydia stood up and climbed to the very top of the bison's head, stretching her nose far into the air and sniffing the breeze. She looked up and down either side of the river making note of the flow of the water. "We must travel up river." She said confidently.

"What is it you smell?" Toby asked, impressed by her skill.

"It is more about what I don't smell. And that is peanuts. If we do not smell peanuts in late summer, we are too far down river."

Timothy looked at Toby with a glowing smile. He was

impressed with his guide and always enjoyed learning new things. Toby on the other hand was puzzled and asked, "what is a peanut?"

Lydia got excited, "Oh, I will show you, they are quite the treat and one of the primary reasons our family crosses the great barrier during the summer."

The team lurched up the river avoiding the sandy embankments and staying on the high side of the eastern bank. They walked for most of the afternoon, following the curvy path of the river until the rough terrain opened up to a field. They stood at a row of long barbed wire fences and Toby stuck his nose in the air sniffing the warm breeze.

"What is that smell?" He asked, smelling something new in the air.

"That, my long tailed friend, is peanuts." Lydia said excitedly and jumped off of the bison sliding down to the ground and running under the fence into the field.

"Wait here friend." Timothy asked Ulysses as he quickly followed Lydia. Toby was right behind him. Ulysses was already grazing the tall grasses that surrounded the fence line.

They entered into a large open field of eerily straight rowed plants. As they walked through the rows for a bit, Lydia started grabbing the brown husks hanging off the plants and tossing them toward the other two. Toby picked up the brown dusty orb and looked it over. "What is it?" He asked as he sniffed it.

"That is a peanut! Take as much as you can carry." They harvested as many goobers as they could get their hands on and made their way back to Ulysses who was happily munching on the tall grasses just outside the fence. When they got outside the fence Lydia tossed her haul of peanuts to the ground. She looked up at Timothy who followed her lead and dropped his peanuts.

"Can you open them up?" She looked down at his sword. Timothy took out his blade and stabbed at the peanut. He struggled to stab at its awkward shape and the shell of the peanut was oddly difficult to slice. Lydia giggled, enjoying seeing the brave mouse who knew so much struggle with such a simple task. "Well, it was worth a try, let me show you how my family opens them." With that, Lydia picked up a small peanut and smashed it against a rock on the ground. She did this repeatedly, occasionally looking at the shell to see her progress. Finally an opening was made in the shell large enough for a peanut to roll out and fall to the ground.

Lydia picked up the nut and split it into two, handing each half to Timothy and Toby. "Here, this is a peanut. Give it a try." They each took a moment to sniff the nut and then proceeded to cram it into their hungry mouths. Timothy's eyes lit up. It was one of the best things he had ever tasted. It brought back memories of his old friend Philip the pack rat. Specifically an old jar that he would sleep in at night, filled with soft bits of fabric and shredded papers. These nuts produced a familiar aroma. For Toby though, there was nothing at all familiar about this exotic and robust flavor. "This is amazing!" Toby spouted out, spitting bits of peanut from his smacking lips.

"We better get to cracking the rest, the sun will set soon. And we don't want to walk along the human path during the night." Lydia said, looking toward the sun lingering low in the sky.

Ulysses looked down at the three who were beginning to tap their peanuts on the rocky ground. Still chewing large stalks of wild grass he spoke up proudly. "Let me show you some bison magic." As he reached his overgrown hoof toward the pile of nuts and gently pressed down. With a single crunch he freed the majority of the peanuts from their shells. Everyone had a laugh and then proceeded to gobble up the loose nuts. Ulysses returned to his grass, chomping loudly. They consumed what they could and packed up the remaining pieces into their cheeks and around Lydia's cargo. Timothy, thinking about how tough the shells were, grabbed a few larger bits thinking it could make a good protective armor if he had the opportunity to sew them into something.

Feeling nourished our adventures pressed on down the fence line until they came to a narrow rocky road. From there they followed the setting sun and pressed forward until they came to a large man made structure that seemed to cross the entire expanse of the river below. As they passed, the ground felt unusually solid below their feet and they could hear the rushing river below them. Human structures were so alien to forest dwelling creatures that most animals found it unsettling, but not Timothy. He was enthralled with the achievement.They were a little past half way when they could see and hear a mechanical beast coming far down the path ahead. They all ran as fast as they could to get to the end of the bridge and off of the human pathway. Ulysses' limp was very pronounced as he hobbled off the bridge and out into the foliage just off the pathway. Everyone rushed, everyone but Timothy who could not help but stare at the mechanical beast coming towards them. It was easily twice the size of Ulysses. Green and yellow in color with a long snout and enormous wheels that crushed the gravel beneath it as it pressed towards them. Everyone else was safely deep into the woods when it passed, all but Timothy who stood at the edge of the treeline and watched intently, looking at how the human riding atop seemed to guide the beast down the path.

As they regrouped in the woods Lydia spoke up with concern. "We are not far from the great barrier. Perhaps a half a day's walk, maybe less." As she glanced over at Ulysses who was struggling to find a comfortable position and sure footing. "We best not attempt to pass the barrier at night. It is a great deal more dangerous at this time of evening."

"I also must rest my weary bones." Ulysses added.

The Epic Of Timothy Gray

They all agreed to settle in for the night. Ulysses circled a clear spot finally falling forward to his knees while letting out a groan as he fully lowered himself to the ground. Everyone else did the same and settled out a soft place to lay their heads. The sky above was growing dark and the stars were hiding behind heavy clouds.

Chapter Fourteen
To Know The Truth

As they lay there spread out under the open sky, tree branches encircling their view of the dimly lit clouds above, Ulysses began to speak. "I have dreamed much about one day returning to my herd. Hard to believe we will cross the barrier tomorrow and I will again enter into the land of my fathers."

Toby inquired, "How long has it been since you were last home?"

"Home? Such a funny thing to call it. I only wish I believed it to be so. Most of my herd did. Unfortunately, I saw the truth and I allowed it to fester in my mind."

Timothy was intrigued, "What was the truth?"

"That our home was a cage. A human trap. Beautiful and lush with vegetation for sure. All our needs, provided for, not a predator in sight, and yet we were daily outnumbered by humans who would challenge our sovereignty and treat us as a spectacle. And if you traveled in any direction for long enough, you would encounter a boundary. I came to understand the truth, that we were indeed captive and not free. This is what drove me to escape. I pursued my freedom because life that is not free is no life at all."

"And if you return, will you not surrender back your freedom?" Timothy asked sincerely.

"It was only after I pursued my freedom that I learned an even deeper truth. That freedom without family is the worst prison one can reside in." The bison responded, looking longingly into the sky. "I was right about everything. We did live in a cage. But given the choice between being right and just letting it go and being happy, I chose to be right, and I have regretted it ever since." The bison looked down to his new friends, "when given the choice, just choose to be happy."

Lydia spoke up, "I too look forward to seeing my family again. And this cargo I return with will save our home and food supply. If you think peanuts are good, you should try our family's blackberry bush."

Ulysses looked down at Timothy and asked, "What do you look forward to upon crossing the great barrier?"

Timothy looked up to Ulysses and then back down to the dirt and after taking a deep breath responded, "I come to balance the scales of suffering. I hope to find the horned owls who killed my family and repay them for the burden of loss that I have come to carry."

Everyone grew silent at his heavy sorrowful words. Then Lydia spoke up, "And after that?"

"I see no path ahead of me that continues on past vengeance. I have come to accept that what I come to do will likely require all that I am."

There was a long contemplative silence that was broken when Toby announced, "I think I would like to try a black berry."

Suddenly a bright flash of light streaked across the sky and a few moments later the crack of thunder. Sparse drops of rain began to fall from the sky onto our unusual group of friends. Ulysses lifted his head and invited them closer, "Come seek shelter beneath me for my coat sheds the rain so well that I cannot feel it."

They all curled up under the great bison's chin and he closed his eyes, head looking forward and ever so regal. Lydia laid close with Timothy and whispered softly, "You know, if you do complete your goal and would like a place to stay, you would like my family home. It is very peaceful and a fine shelter from danger." She said somewhat questioningly. Timothy heard her well, but chose not to respond and he laid still, pretending to be asleep. "I do hope you think about it." She spoke again softly before rolling over and curling into position to sleep for the night.

Timothy thought about how difficult it was to lose his family, and knowing how dangerous his path was, he was reluctant to allow himself to become entangled in relationships. How could he put someone else through that kind of loss knowing the great heartache it causes. He had already allowed himself to get close with Toby and now continually worried that the dangers ahead or those that pursue them from behind would put his friends' lives at risk. Was he more afraid of losing them or of them losing him? It was all too much to bear. This calling of his was much clearer when he traveled alone.

The gentle rain and occasional thunder was a cool comfort to our travelers and almost masked the distant sound of coyotes howling through the night.

Chapter Fifteen
Making Sacrifices

When the morning came, the sky did not spread out and
allow the sunlight through. Instead the clouds hung heavy
in the sky. The rain had settled into a drizzle but the sky
still echoed thunderous roars from far away. As they set off
in the opposite direction of what they all agreed should be
the sunrise Lydia softly announced, "Now, when we get to
the barrier, we will not be crossing it right away. It's very
important that we do not enter the smooth gray surface until
I have navigated us to the crossing point. The barrier has
many dangers. One being that there is limited cover." She
looked over at Timothy, "which makes us very easy prey for
winged predators. And two, the barrier is much like a human
pathway, but much larger and the human carriers travel at
such speeds that sometimes they seem invisible. They mostly
remain on the smooth surface, so if we stay on rocky earth,

we should be safe. But taking one step across that edge line guarantees death."

Toby and Timothy were unsure quite what to expect but paid close attention hoping that it would all make sense when they arrived. Along the way Ulysses asked Timothy, "Did you hear the coyotes last night?"

"I did." Timothy responded softly not wanting to worry the others.

"They do seem to be on my trail and making better time than we are able. I don't think we can spare another night. If we don't pass the barrier today, we will have to face off with those coyotes again."

"I have been thinking about that." Timothy said, confirming that he shared the same concerns.

"And when that time comes, Do we have a plan?" Ulysses asked.

"The plan is to cross the barrier. Apart from that, we have only our hopes." Timothy tried to encourage him.

"If it comes to it, sacrifices may need to be made." Ulysses stated, looking off into the horizon.

Timothy, unsure of what sacrifices he was referring to, simply responded, "I am hopeful we will find our crossing before it comes to that."

"Do you all hear that?" Toby interjected.

There was a low rumble, like a quiet thunder that would come and go. Like a bumble bee flying by, but repeated and deep. Timothy could almost feel it under his feet through the earth itself. They inquisitively pushed forward through the brush until they stepped into a clearing. The sound became louder and each of them had an instinctive moment of panic when they saw it. It was the great barrier. Like nothing Timothy had ever seen before, it stretched from horizon to horizon, as if God himself had dragged his finger across the surface and drawn a line across the earth. Bright colored metal beasts of all kinds making rumbling growling sounds were moving up and down the barrier in each direction. The sight of it made Timothy feel very small and insignificant, even for a mouse.

Timothy spoke up, "is this the great barrier?"

"Part of it." Ulysses answered, "it goes on forever."

Toby questioned, "forever?"

Ulysses ignored him, because he wasn't even sure if forever was a real thing.

They all lingered there for a moment just processing what

they were seeing, before Ulysses spoke up again, "we should keep moving."

They approached a good vantage point on an elevation above the barrier but close enough to get a good look. Not far away there was a flurry of activity near the side of the roadway. Large turkey vultures hunched over the eviscerated carcass of a deer several days old and putting off the pungent aroma of death.

Lydia looked at her charges who seemed overwhelmed with all they were taking in, "Come, follow me." she gestured while heading northward toward the vultures. "See those lines on the road? Stay far away from them, but we must follow the barrier for quite a way before we get to the safe crossing point."

"How long until we cross the barrier?" Timothy asked, giving Ulysses a glance.

Lydia paused and turned back. "If we make haste, we should be able to cross by tomorrow morning." She answered. "It is forbidden to attempt to cross during the night. It is far too dangerous, especially for our large friend." She answered, giving a nod to Ulysses.

The thunder clapped again and the rain started to pick up. Ulysses looked down at Timothy, "I think it is best that we part ways here. For if I travel with you, my scent will travel with you as well. And this is no place to make a stand against a pack of foes."

"And what will come of you? How will you stand alone?" Timothy objected.

"Worry not friend, I will simply find another way to cross." Ulysses feigned.

"I know of no other way, and if another exists, it is many days farther." Lydia chimed in. "And trust me, to walk across the barrier is certain death", she added gesturing over to the corpse being pulled apart by giant scavenger birds.

"Even so, I am not long for this world. And this way, I will purchase you the opportunity to cross safely. Maybe, if I do get taken out by this human monstrosity, I will take a few of my foes with me." Ulysses smirked.

Timothy pleaded with him, "Friend, do not give up. Our journey is not over."

"Oh courageous mouse, this is not me giving up. This is me, following my hopes." The massive bison said gently with his deep voice looking down eye to eye with Timothy. "Now go, May we meet again on the other side one day." and with that, Ulysses looked up over the ridge to see a coyote watching from the tree line. He snorted a deep breath, stamped his hooves to ensure his footing and he took off in the other direction.

The coyote darted after him and soon two more coyotes came running out of the woods. Ulysses had the advantage of a head start, but the landscape left no place to hide. The coyotes paid no attention to the deer carcass, the vultures, or two mice and an opossum standing not too far from the roadway. They seemed singularly focused on Ulysses.

Timothy was powerless to do anything. No matter how clever he could be, or how skilled he was with his blade, or his veracity in battle, he was still a small mouse with small legs. They all stretched onto their hind legs to see the chase in progress. As the pack of coyotes got closer and began to circle Ulysses' position, Timothy knew it would be over soon. He turned his head and began walking the other direction. "Come now, let us not waste his sacrifice."

The two others were reluctant to look away, but they also knew that Timothy was right. They glanced back a few times but then reached pace with Timothy marching forward.

As they got closer to the vultures tearing at the now rotted deer flesh, the birds flapped their wings to demonstrate their size and power. Timothy unsheathed his blade. "It's alright Timothy, they only eat the flesh of the dead, which is plentiful out here." Lydia placed her hand on Timothy to ease his nerves. Timothy was upset. He almost wanted an excuse to use his blade. He wanted to do something, anything, other than just walk along this road and think about his new friend being slaughtered behind them.

"Timothy Gray?" said the vulture, whose red face was hunched between his high shoulders standing on the body of the decaying deer.

Timothy froze in place and placed his hand back on the hilt of his blade. "Who are you and how do you know my name?"

"Everyone knows your name, small mouse. It has been whispered on the breeze. You who come to kill the horned owl." the vulture spoke in an accusatory tone.

"And would you try to stop me?" Timothy took a stance, prepared to fight.

"I would never get in the way of one animal killing another." The vulture laughed. "That is how I survive in this world of death. But be warned small mouse, for they too know you are coming." The other vultures now all looked at Timothy, all wanting to square up the mouse of legend. For a moment they all just glared at each other, but the tension was broken by a loud noise followed by more loud noises. Sounds Timothy had not heard, but reminded him of the honk of the goose when it was terrified. Then screeching and more honking. The vultures, almost on pure instinct flapped their wings and took to the air.

Everyone turned back where they had come from to see in the far distance that Ulysses was venturing out into the barrier. The coyotes had broken away their pursuit as they too knew the barrier was forbidden to enter and would lead to death. Yet something strange happened. Something Lydia would later recall as the oddest thing she had ever seen at the great barrier. As Ulysses walked onto the roadway, the monstrous metal beasts that would normally just smash through any creature came to a halt. Humans stepped out of their metal trappings and almost with a sense of reverence looked on as Ulysses crossed their path. One by one humans stopped and watched as Ulysses jumped the middle barrier and walked across the massive road. The line of metal beasts had gotten longer and longer until the ones passing by Timothy began to slow down too. Just when Timothy began to wonder if they should attempt to cross too, out of nowhere more came from the other direction. Timothy was startled. He looked back to see Ulysses walking into the tree line on the other side of the barrier, safe and without harm.

The coyotes were infuriated. One of them saw an opening and attempted to pursue and cross the barrier himself. After all, they stopped for the bison. But that coyote was quick to learn, the metal beasts do not stop for much. A cracking sound could be heard from far away as the coyote on the road was sent spinning. It yelped in agony and just as quickly went quiet and limp. Other metal beasts moved around to avoid it at first, but then soon a massive one just plowed right through crushing the coyote. His companions stood at the edge of the roadway frantically watching and weeping, crying out to their lost friend as if to beckon him to come back. To which he did not reply, nor could he. Lydia was right. To venture into the barrier was instant death, but somehow,

Ulysses was given a pass. Maybe because of his massive size, or maybe Timothy thought, it was because the humans, like Timothy, had never seen a bison before. Maybe Ulysses was more special than even they had realized.

"Come on now, we can not linger long in these open spaces." Lydia gestured to them to follow as she looked to the skies above. The thunder cracked again and as they pressed on down the barrier the rains began to fall heavier upon them.

The Epic Of Timothy Gray

Chapter Sixteen
The Balanced Scales

As they continued on, the barrier became narrowed by massive cliff edges on either side. Every so often they would pass another rotting carcass of an animal that had entered the barrier. Armadillo, raccoon, opossum, squirrel, and some so mangled and destroyed that they were no longer recognizable. Timothy was disturbed by how this human magic seemed so cold and evil, just heaping suffering onto all who come across it. Killing not for food, nor for survival, but for some purpose outside of Timothy's grasp. It made no sense, but at the same time, it was familiar to him. Being in the habit of having read the occasional newspaper before they were used to start fires in the hunting cabin, Timothy had read about these massive human projects, but a black and white photo on the third page of the newspaper could not convey the massive size of this undertaking. As they travelled up one of the cliff edges on narrow pathways to avoid getting too close to the barrier, they came up to a post on the side of the road. Timothy paused and read it aloud, "Interstate Oklahoma 35".

"Is that what it says?" Lydia asked.

"Yes, but what that means, I have no idea. This here is a darker magic than I have ever studied." Timothy answered, wanting to distance himself from human magic, now that he had seen where it leads. This must be what the soul of the forest was referring to. Timothy had never before been ashamed of human accomplishment. He was only inspired by it. Humans could accomplish anything they desired. Only now he was realizing that with limitless potential, how important it was to have righteous desire. For what good were all the stories of nobility and honor that Timothy had come to love and admire in the face of this heinous display of cold injustice. Unlike other human magic which brought structure to the chaos of nature, this had gone full circle and through its brute structure, sewed chaos to everything that came into contact with it. Maybe human magic was corrupting. Everything Timothy had believed was being called into question.

As they crossed a narrow ledge, a rockface to their right and to their left a long drop on a steep surface down to the barrier line. The rain had made the rocky path slippery and water was running down the cliff edge across their path making it difficult to find good footing. Lydia led the way with Toby behind her and Timothy taking up the rear deep in thought. Suddenly, Toby's hind leg slipped sending his back side slipping down the steep edge toward the barrier. Timothy sprung to action grabbing the bit of string tied around Toby, still attached to the pack of cargo around his back. Timothy used it to steady Toby who was hanging on to the narrow rock way with all his might.

"I have you, friend." Timothy said bracing himself and supporting Toby using the strap of bison hair as best he could. Toby scurried up the cliff and got his hind legs back on sure footing. "We are almost out of this, it will level out here soon." Lydia said to encourage them. She wanted to be a good guide, but she had never traveled with larger companions before. It was a good thing Ulysses found his own way, because there was no way he could have made this part of the journey, she thought.

As they continued the ground became more level and easy to traverse. Suddenly a burst of activity fluttered about as dozens of small sparrows descended upon them circling them and bouncing back and forth around them. "Timothy Gray! Timothy Gray!" they repeated his name bouncing with excitement. They almost spoke as one entity but each continuing the thought of the other, "She calls upon you", "the queen of the parliament", "leader of the horned owls", "she calls upon you", "she wishes to meet", "to discuss your terms", "she is afraid".. And with that last statement all the sparrows looked upon the one who blurted it out with a look of shock and concern. Then they all burst apart flying away leaving the one who said she was afraid. It looked around concerned and then spoke up, "just ahead of your path in the tree line she awaits" and jumped to flight leaving our trio behind.

Timothy, nor any of his companions had a moment to react let alone say anything. Timothy took a moment and reflected on his journey. He considered his singular purpose and replayed in his mind the tragic loss of his family. The slow flapping of large owl wings in the tree of his ancestors and the mangled remains of his brothers and sisters, his mother. He boiled with rage looking into the treeline ahead of him.

"Timothy, are we to go and fight now?" Toby said nervously. "I have no Excalibur. I only have these delicate claws and my teeth." Timothy thought about his many previous battles. He remembered back long before he had met Toby of how he took on a hawk and barely escaped death. He knew of the fear involved in standing up to powerful tyrants and he knew that fear would be too much for poor Toby.

"It is mad to stand up against the queen of the horned owls. This is not what I volunteered for." Lydia contested.

"Listen friends, I must go alone. Besides, Toby, you have seen how I have defeated an owl before. I need her to lower her guard. It will be her over confidence that will be her downfall. You all keep going and wait for me at the next ridge. Wait for me only a little while and if hope falters, continue on without me."

"But Timothy..." Toby began to plead.

"We must fulfill our obligation to Lydia and her family, Toby. Brave Toby. Make sure her cargo gets to her family. Will you do that for me?" Timothy asked placing a hand under Toby's chin to lift it up.

"Yes friend." Toby perked up, He had never thought of himself as brave. "I will make sure of it."

Timothy turned to Lydia, "My lady, it has been an honor." As he bowed and took her hand in his, he laid a gentle kiss upon it.

Lydia was at a loss for words. Not only because of how odd it was to be kissed on the hand, because this was clearly a human gesture and not one she had ever experienced, but also because it touched her deeply and made her feel a level of respect and appreciation that she had never experienced as a lowly field mouse. She blushed and her whiskers trembled.

Timothy turned, straightened up his garments and began tramping off toward the treeline. It did occur to him that this could be a trap. Timothy thought himself a master of traps. He began weaving his approach and grew cautious of his surroundings. The grass was tall and covered his position and the falling rain dampened the sound of his approach, but as he entered under the canopy of the treeline, the grass grew shorter and the rain sounds shifted to high on the broad leaves above. He paused there and looked ahead, seeing a clearing surrounded by trees and just ahead of that clearing an enormous horned owl sat perched on the branch of an old burned tree that only possessed the singular branch. It was a terrible position for him to approach from. But the more he thought about it, the owl too was in a terrible position. Her eyes closed, she sat in on the lowest branch in the wooded area. He could consider many ways of attack and many better positions from which to defend. Perhaps she really did want to meet. After some consideration, Timothy decided that the most appropriate action would be to walk into this clearing, courageous and unafraid. Perhaps she is afraid. Timothy's only fear presently was not seeing his friends again. Thinking about disappointing them as they waited for him. But he knew his journey would end at some point. Too often he escaped by mere luck and coincidence. He would once again take his chances with fate and let the gods decide.

Timothy took in a deep breath and held his head high as he walked confidently out into the clearing. Not turning his head, but paying close attention to his peripheral view he stepped forward and stood dead center in the clearing just a short sprint distance away from the owl. His hand rested on the tang of his blade. It was quiet other than the tapping of rain on the leaves above and the owl's eyes were still closed when she suddenly spoke. "You must be the fabled mouse." Her eyes sprang open so quickly that it made Timothy question if they had been open all along. Her eyes were large and dark, swallowing up the light in this dimly lit wooded sanctuary.

"I am Timothy Gray." he announced confidently.

"Timothy Gray, slayer of owls, foxes, and snakes." She exclaimed. "The magic wielding mouse who rides bison, feeds bears, practices the dark arts of the humans. The tiny mouse who has single handedly united the forest in a spirit of revolt against the laws of nature."

Timothy wasn't sure how to respond. She seemed to know everything about him and his journey and it was unsettling to him.

"I have lived long enough to have learned not to believe everything you hear on the forest breeze. So I thought it best to ask you here to confirm. Are you truly here to kill me?"

Timothy was taken back by the direct question. This was not what he was expecting. "You and your kind, yes." he responded.

"My kind?" She scoffed. "Do you know how many of my kind there are?"

Timothy looked around, expecting there to be more here than the one before him.

"Poor little mouse. You fight a battle in which the victor has already been decided and you don't even realize." she said as she closed her eyes and turned her head. Her head slowly spun around until she faced the other direction.

"Did you invite me here to face me in battle?" Timothy said feeling disrespected that she turned her head away.

Her head swiveled back slowly, "I invited you here to see if you were a mouse or if you indeed were consumed by the evils of man."

"Do not lecture me on evil. You slayed my entire family." Timothy said, growing angry.

"Those were dark times, small mouse." The owl's voice grew soft and its eyes shifted downward. "And I do remember... for how could I forget."

Timothy was confused. The owl seemed sad, its eyes full of remorse. This was far from what he was expecting. The thought crossed his mind that she was putting on a show and simply trying to manipulate him.

"You were not the only one who experienced loss on that day." She said looking up toward the great barrier in the distance. "What I am about to share with you, I wish only to share once, so listen carefully. I want not to relive it again."

"This land on which you stand has been the home of my kind

for many generations. The day you lost your family is also the day I lost mine."

"Everything we knew was gone in a flash. And the great thunder that many claim to have heard, it took our hearing from us. For days after, all we heard was the ringing. We could not communicate. Many of us had lost nests and young owlets in the preceding seasons of tree falls. But the day the forest was cleared with the great explosions that cleared the pathway for the great barrier, on that day we were forced to flee, for our very survival, but without the ability to understand each other. We were lost in our own minds. Afraid and hostile to the outside world as it had been so extremely hostile toward us."

The great horned owl looked down and away from Timothy. "I am truly sorry for what happened at the tree of your home. I know it means nothing to feel regret about such things. I know you have come a long way to exact your revenge and I don't expect you to have sympathy on me and spare my life. But do want you to see and know that this human magic you embrace to exact your revenge, is the very thing that has caused such suffering for all of us to bear."

Timothy was conflicted. She seemed so sincere. Such a different creature than he encountered in the tree of his childhood home. He did have sympathy for her. He looked down at his cloak and sword. He thought about the lives he had taken. Some in defense of his life or others, but some needlessly. He thought about the owl he hunted and murdered simply to make a boat from its feathers. Had he become the monster he pursued?

He looked up at the owl, "And what now? What would you have us do? Forgive and forget!?"

"Oh small mouse, I am sure we will face off one day to the death. For I still need to eat and I don't know if you have enough mouse left in you to comprehend forgiveness. But I hope that when that day comes, I face a true mouse and not this pawn of man's wizardry that stands before me."

She spun her head side to side checking the perimeter. "That is if the human's dark magic doesn't get me first. Every season we face a slaughter to the great barrier. I have witnessed it myself as my mate made the mistake of seeking prey through the trees only to enter the barrier and be shattered into a dust of feather and blood. This magic is darker than you know and it spreads across creation, devouring it. Man's magic knows no limits. And we suffer at their latitude. We face annihilation at every turn, so pardon me if I choose not to fear you, small mouse."

She spread her wings and instantly grew to a massive size triggering a deep childlike fear inside Timothy. She shook the water off of her plumage, spraying droplets all about, she flapped her wings majestically and took to the air in an eerie silence. She soared away leaving Timothy standing alone in the clearing, raindrops falling all around.

Timothy wasn't sure what to make of all of this. He was

conflicted... disappointed... disheartened... but at the same time he was swept over with relief at the thought of catching up with his friends. So he took off out of the woods and onward toward the bluffs ahead where the barrier cut through the landscape. His thought reflecting on the worry and concern in his friends eyes when last they spoke and now his one solace in all of this drama surrounding his existence was the idea that seeing his companions again would bring joy to their faces and this singular thought became his focus.

The Epic Of Timothy Gray

Chapter Seventeen

Danger at Every Turn

Timothy caught up with his companions and the expression on their faces did exactly for Timothy's heart what was needed. Toby smiled ear to ear as he was known to do. Lydia was so excited to see him again that she hugged his neck and placed a kiss on his cheek. Which surprised and thrilled Timothy more than he knew how to express. He told his friends of the owl and her words. He looked upon the sharp edges of the canyon forged by man to contain the great barrier and told them about the claimed history of it all.

"So, what will you do then Timothy? Are we still hunting your enemies?" Toby asked supportively.

Timothy paused and looked down contemplatively. "I am

unsure at this time who my enemies are." he said, "But one thing I am sure of" as he looked up at Toby, "is that I know who my friends are."

Lydia perked up excitedly, "We are almost there!" she pointed ahead to a bridge that went across the great barrier. They had been walking the length of the barrier the better part of the day and the sun was setting beneath the thick dark sky causing the slightest of orange and pink colors to line the edges of the dark rain clouds above. "If we hurry, we may even be able to cross before it is too dark." Lydia screamed as she took off running across the field to where the bridge met a small human pathway leading through the woods. The two others followed her lead, chasing her through the field. The rain had lightened up as bars of sunlight shot through the sky from the setting sun, providing the most illustrious array of colors in the sky. For the first time in a while, Timothy felt hopeful. Not just about their journey but about life. He had learned to accept his life of solitude. He had adapted to his trauma and so fixated on his revenge that the possibility of relationships and finding family again had been out of his perception. But here he was, frolicking in a field with a large smile on his face.

Just then a sound pierced the evening sky sending chills down his spine. A howl from a coyote. And not a distant howl, but eerily close by. Far too close to not send shivers of fear down the spine of a small forest animal. Their frolic run turned into a frantic one. Timothy turned to see two coyotes looking directly toward them from the tree line.

Their position was clear and the grass was not tall enough to hide their escape. The two hounds set forth in pursuit. Just as the team reached the small human path on the top of the hill there was a slight amount of concealment behind the wall forming the bridge over the great barrier which they could take shelter behind, but would not protect them from attack.

Timothy turned to his friends hiding behind the wall. There was no cover on this bridge. It was a strategic death trap. High walls on either side enclosed them in, and even if one could jump over would lead to a quick death on the barrier below. Even if the fall didn't kill you, the passing traffic would finish you off. Timothy was decisive as ever and knew instantly that his dream of family and friends was a hope that would need to be dashed on the rocks of reason. Timothy quickly removed the cargo from Toby to lighten his load and pushed Lydia onto his back.

"Toby, you must go now, do not hesitate. Get her across. I will slow them down" Timothy pleaded.

Toby hesitated, "But we will not make it. I cannot face these foes alone. I have no weapon and I am not a skilled fighter." Toby was frozen in fear breathing in short bursts.

"Listen to me Toby, you are not alone." Timothy pulled his blade from its sheath and placed it in Toby's hands. "Take this, it is the greatest of human magic and it will protect you both."

Toby took the sword into his hands and looked into it seeing his own reflection in the metal blade. He looked at the words engraved on its side and said out loud "Excalibur?"

Timothy grabbed Toby by the arm, "You must be brave, friend, trust in the magic and it will protect you." With that, Timothy picked up the cargo satchel and hoisted over his shoulder. "Now Go! Trust in the magic and in me my friend."

Toby placed the blade in his mouth to hold it and took off running down the side of the bridge going over the great barrier. By this time a great many crows had lined up on the bridge watching for the drama to unfold. Maybe they wanted to witness how the story ended or maybe they just wanted to make a quick meal out of the vanquished remains of battle. Timothy took the large satchel and dragged it out to the middle of the path of the entrance to the bridge. This of all places felt like a fitting place to make one last stand. For his honor and for his friends. He placed the cargo down and stood atop of it, making himself stand out. When the coyotes came around the corner and saw him there it did make them stop and take notice.

"Stop there, cursed dog!" Timothy yelled, getting their full attention. It worked. They didn't see as Toby crested the peak of the bridge, Lydia holding tightly onto his back as he ran with all his might. By the time the coyotes started inching closer Toby was fully out of view and heading to the other side.

The coyotes growled with heads low to the ground as each took a flanking position on either side of Timothy. They lowered their bodies ready to pounce when Timothy spoke up again. "I will warn you no further, you have chosen to engage in battle with the one and only Timothy Gray. Wizard of dark human magic and mighty warrior of the sword!" Timothy spoke deep and loud and gestured to his sheath as though to prepare to draw his blade. At the sound of his name the coyotes went silent and took pause, one even stepped backward ever so slightly. They looked at each other and then back at Timothy. The crows all around began to caw and hop in place as if to entice the drama. They all knew his name. If Timothy had learned anything on his journey thus far, it was that word travels long and wide in the forest and that a story, though sometimes true and sometimes exaggerated, is a powerful thing that only grows stronger each time it is shared. The coyotes took a more defensive stance as the one closest began to speak. "So it is you. You are the one to blame for our meal escaping us. We had worn him down for weeks and then he came across your path and suddenly the chase was all new."

"So you have heard of my great powers? How I split a snake in two? How I single handedly defeated a fox? Why then would you test me now in this dark hour? Do you wish to die?" Timothy again bluffed with confidence.

"I have heard the stories, little mouse." spoke the coyote, while the other coyote continued to back away, spooked by the legend and the crows who continued to gather in numbers and cawing loudly. "And I know what a story is... just the musing of birds gossiping in the wind" he snarled, taking a step closer. "I trust not in the gossip of birds. I trust my senses. And you know what I smell right now?" He took another step closer, now cowering over Timothy. "I smell fear."

Timothy knew his ruse was used up. His only hope was that the shells of peanuts in the cargo were strong enough to protect him now. The coyote began to growl and lower his stance again ready to pounce. Timothy quickly dove down and retrieved a couple shells placing them over his hands. Just as quickly as he moved, the coyote dove toward him, snipping at him. He lifted the shells over his head instinctively cowering in fear down into the cargo satchel. The next thing he knew, he was in complete darkness and felt a sharp pain in his ankle. He could barely make out the gnashing teeth surrounding him. Timothy had been taken into the mouth of the coyote and was now being chewed upon, nut shells were cracking around him. They did not slow the coyote down but instead encouraged it, thinking it was breaking the bones of the small mouse within its mouth. Suddenly Timothy's eyes burned and it became hard to breathe. This felt like death. No, maybe not. This felt worse than death. Timothy felt pain all over before being spat onto the cold wet ground below. Covered in warm wetness that he couldn't determine if it was saliva from the coyote or his own blood, Timothy was blind and gasping for air. The end could not come soon enough. As he felt his breath labor and attempted to open his eyes, he could hear the coyote above him with jaw open wide, drooling all over him. Then as he forced his eyes open all he could see was a blinding light and a loud clap of what he could only process as being the jaws of the coyote taking his life.

The Epic Of Timothy Gray

Chapter Eighteen
The Death of Timothy Gray

Timothy awoke in a strange place. He stood on his hind legs. He looked at his hands and body; he was naked without his clothing and belt. But he touched his face and felt the length of his ears. He was somehow in one piece. How was any of this possible, he thought. Looking around he could see nothing, just a pinkish fog and red ground that felt firm beneath him but was a dark red color, like blood.

"Am I dead?" he thought out loud. He heard his own words in a muffled sort of way, but the air was thick and seemed to silence all sound. He was surrounded by a dark nothingness, and it chilled him to the bone.

If he was dead, then how was he here? Timothy had read

a great many books covering a great deal of human magic, mostly concerned with efforts to not die. He had never read anything much about life after death. Although there was a story he did read once, about a friend who called his dead friend out of the grave, and his friend did come out, Oh what was that old and tattered book and how Timothy wished now he had read it entirely. Timothy was introduced to the rough idea of heaven and hell, but had never given it much consideration. He had seen with his own eyes how animals rest their bones into the earth and bugs and nature reclaim their bodies. That was always comfort enough without considering a life after death, but here he stood. In a very unreal, real place. He felt both hot and cold at the same time. He tried to speak again, "Where am I?" but as the words came out of his mouth, his mouth burned with heat he had never known. Surely this was hell.

If it was hell, he did belong here. He had spent his whole life selfishly pursuing his own desires, practicing human magic, exacting his revenge and rage on every predatory animal he came across since the loss of his family. Timothy realized that he was a ball of selfish desires that he had never kept in check. Even now, knowing that the owls who caused his suffering were suffering themselves, he could not and would not forgive.

Forgiveness. A word that now felt heavy on his mind. There was much about it in that book he didn't finish where that man walked away from the grave. What a story he now wishes he understood the details of. Yes, if this is hell, he was in the right place. His head felt strange and the fog seemed to penetrate his soul, blurring not only his vision but his perception of reality.

Suddenly in front of him stood a tall noble creature. A dog. Not like the coyote who had killed him, but a more regal beast. Clean and well kept with white fur almost glowing in purity. The dog was still. Not panting or moving a muscle, but its eyes looked down toward Timothy. "Am I in hell?" Timothy inquired of the dog. The dog's mouth did not move, but a voice could be heard.

"It is what you make of it." the voice boomed from above.

"Are you the creator?" Timothy asked, fearing the answer.

It did not answer his question, but posed one back in return. "Who are you little one?" the voice said compassionately.

"I am Timothy Gray. Who are you?" Timothy asked, trembling in fear.

"I am here to guide you to your path Timothy Gray." The dog looked down, still not moving its lips but now staring directly into Timothy's soul. "Are you a man or are you a mouse?"

Timothy stepped back confused and there before him on the red ground laid two divergent lines coming out from underneath him. One white and one as black as the darkest night. The two paths stretched away from either side of the dog standing in the middle looking down at Timothy.

Timothy looked down each path and then back to the dog, "I just want an end to my suffering! You tell me what I am!" The dog looked up away from Timothy and a voice spoke firm but softly as it faded and echoed into the darkness. "Only you can determine your path, but there is no path which does not pass through suffering." Timothy became angry, "Why!? Why am I doomed to suffer! What purpose is there in it!?"

The dog looked down at Timothy again, its face expressing compassion. "The One who brings the rain and causes the flood waters to rise is the same One who causes the sun to shine and brings up food from the earth." The voice spoke softly and quietly as if it was fading into the fog. A tear fell from the dog's eye and hit the ground in front of Timothy. "Pain does not exist to inspire more pain, my small furry one. Pain exists so that healing may begin something new." The voice was now a whisper. "Are you a man or are you a mouse?"

Timothy was shaken. He looked down each path, unsure where they led him. This all felt like a dream or a nightmare. He knew he was a mouse, but he knew he was also more. Timothy fell down to his knees and wept. "I do not know!" his tears fell down to the path below him as he lowered his head and screamed "WHAT AM I?"

When he raised his head, the dog was gone. He looked down where his hand had touched the ground and felt his tear fall to the ground splashing onto the white path. More and more drops began to fall all around, and as they did, the path began to bleed its white color and the dark path too seemed to bleed away until the two met in the middle, combining to reveal a gray pathway leading straight where the dog had been. A path that wasn't there before now became more and more distinct as the rain washed away the other two pathways. Timothy was deeply moved by this revelation and took a step forward onto the path. He could have sworn he heard the voice of Lydia down the pathway, but he couldn't make out what she was saying. He started taking another step forward, and another until he heard her voice clearly saying, "It will be alright Timothy, take my hand, it will be alright."

Timothy darted forward down the path with all his might stretching his hand out and screaming, "Please, please, SAVE ME!"

The Epic Of Timothy Gray

Chapter Nineteen
The Rise of a Hero

Toby and Lydia had made it safely to the other side of the
bridge. Toby got into the cover of nearby brush just off
the pathway and pulled the sword out of his mouth. It just
dawned on him that this sword had given him the courage to
be decisive and save Lydia, but it also became clear in his gut
that he had left Timothy defenseless. He took heavy breaths
trying to figure out what to do. After brief contemplation, he
remembered the time he last thought he had died and had
awoken to Timothy sleeping at his side. He could not bear
to leave his friend behind who had stuck by his side in the
face of danger. Toby turned to Lydia, "Stay here, find cover,
I will return and take you home." Lydia grabbed his arm and
pleaded with him. "Be careful Toby."

Toby took the blade back into his mouth and darted back

up the bridge. He reached the other side of the bridge just in time to see his friend getting devoured by the coyote. The coyote had taken in Timothy and the cargo satchel all in one large bite and was attempting to chew him up. Snapping and thrashing what was in his mouth. Toby at that moment felt driven by a sense of justice and rage he had never known before. He took the blade into his hand and ran over in front of the coyote who was now writhing and choking on Timothy. Toby spoke firmly but not too loud as to alert the other coyote. "Let my friend go!" he demanded, pointing the blade at the coyote who was now clearly struggling greatly with what was in his mouth. The coyote's eyes were watering, and mucus was coming from its nose and mouth like it had instantly caught an awful disease.

Suddenly the coyote spat Timothy and the satchel of cargo from his mouth. Toby was surprised that it was so obedient to his demand until Toby's eyes also began to water. There was a poison of sorts in the air. Toby took a step back and looked down at the ground where his friend laid writhing in agony. Timothy's leg had been bitten clean off, but worse than that, the peppers that were in the satchel cargo had spilled out and were opened up. It was burning the air between them. The coyote was in agony but also appalled by Toby's stance against him. As it spat and drooled and walked over above Timothy opening its mouth wide to show its teeth to Toby it drooled over Timothy and the cargo satchel.

As Toby looked deep into the eyes of the predator who was about to chew his face off, realizing that other than holding this blade, he knew not how to fight with it. He trembled with fear but then saw an odd thing. There was a light in the coyote's eyes. A brightening light that changed the perception of expression from rage, to fear. The light grew bright, so bright that it was blinding and Toby ducked down to shelter his friend from attack. That is when a loud roar of a human metal beast drove right over Toby at high-speed smashing into the face of the coyote who puffed into a pink mist of blood and hair rolling underneath the human vehicle which did not even begin to slow down. By the time Toby got back up, there laid before him was a mangled coyote and the back end of a human truck driving away into the darkness. Toby was quick to remember the other coyote was not far away. He grabbed Timothy and tossed him over his shoulder, but instead of running away, he did what he thought Timothy would do. He ran toward the danger. He came up to the mangled corpse of the coyote and stood atop of it. The other coyote had run into the bush to avoid the truck and was now returning up the path to the bridge. Upon seeing Toby standing atop of his fallen comrade, he took a step back. Toby shouted. "Be amazed and terrified at my human magic!" as he pointed his sword at the last remaining coyote. "My name is Tobias Greenbottom and I will smite thee with my deadly magic!" Toby screamed to the top of his lungs. The crows were almost cheering in unison now and flapping their wings.

The last coyote knew what he had seen. He saw a tiny mouse of fabled legend take out the leader of his pack and he didn't dare take on the dark wizardry of his companions. He tucked his tail between his legs and quickly turned and ran away.

The Epic Of Timothy Gray

Toby took Timothy upon his back and went back across the bridge to where Lydia waited. The crows jumped from their perch to the corpse of the coyote below and began to feast on his spread-out entrails.

Toby was gagging at this point from the peppers and crying not only from the burning smell but the idea that his friend may already be dead. When they got to Lydia, she helped wash him in puddles of rainwater that had formed near the roadway. "Quickly, we must get away from the human pathways at night, they are very dangerous." Lydia said as she laid Timothy on Toby's back and then climbed aboard to keep cleaning him. Toby took off with the two balanced on his back. He could hear Lydia speaking softly to Timothy, weeping over him, stroking his face. "It will be alright Timothy, take my hand, it will be alright." as she took his hand in hers Timothy squeezed it tight. His whole body seemed to jerk as he yelled out loud, "Please, please, SAVE ME!"

"Oh Timothy!" She hugged him hard. He was still blind but he was now gasping for air as she stroked his fur and kept comforting him. "We have you, friend. You are okay."

Chapter Twenty
Life Anew

The rest of the journey was a blur to Timothy. He remembered being cared for by Lydia and watching a blurry sky shake back and forth as he rode atop his best friend's back. He could hear the voices of strangers and distinctly remembered hearing familiar voices too. He was given drink and food, and he was groomed and looked after like he hadn't been since he was a young mouse. He could hear the recounting of stories with added theatricality by the time summer had reached its end, he had begun to see clearly again.

He awoke on a crisp chill morning to the sweet fresh air. He was in a shallow burrow surrounded by his things. His garments laid up on a rock nearby and his sword resting in some bits of bark that were tied together with string. The sunlight poked in through the opening of the burrow and he could hear the voices of young pup mice playing and family in joyous conversation. Timothy sat up in bed and began to move. Right away he noticed his left leg was missing. There was a stump where it once was but the stump was healed over, as though someone had been caring for it well. Timothy got up as best he could but had to drag himself out of the hovel, into the daylight. When he crawled out, he was greeted by small pup mouse voices shouting, "He's awake! Timothy's awake!"

A young mouse about the same size as Timothy came over and lifted Timothy, helping him to stand upright. "Come now, we cannot let our hero crawl on the ground." He held Timothy up and wrapped his arm around his shoulder to support him. With his other hand he patted Timothy on the back. "I am Jethro, glad to make your acquaintance."

"I am Timothy Gr..." He interrupted, "Sir, we all know who you are. You are the great Timothy Gray, and the one responsible for bringing my sister home safely." Jethro looked down at Timothy's missing leg, "At great personal sacrifice. You will never crawl here sir, there are always plenty of us around to help carry you."

As they walked out in front of the bush Timothy dared to ask, "Plenty of us?" But before he could get the question out of his mouth he looked around to see at least two dozen mice playing and resting under a large looming blackberry bush.

"Quick, someone fetch Lydia and Tobias" Jethro announced. "They will want to speak with him right away."

Timothy sat there as mice brought him bits of blackberry and offerings of string and small human items they had found, buttons, bolts and bits of paper with words on it. Timothy was still a little dazed but responded with gratitude. When Toby and Lydia arrived they ran and embraced their friend. Toby saw the piles of gifts before him and had an epiphany, "I will be right back, I have something for you."

Lydia slowly spoke up, "Are you feeling alright? How is your leg looking?" She looked him up and down and examined his injuries closely. She reached down and felt his leg stump. "Oh, it has healed nicely." she said. Timothy wasn't accustomed to being cared for, let alone the touch of a female. He instinctively reached down to remove her hand from him and with their hands connected she looked up at him and they made eye contact. She smiled warmly at him, and he could not help but do the same. This is what it means to be a mouse, he thought to himself. "Your eyes look much better now; can you see things clearly?" Lydia asked.

"Yes, for the first time in a long time, I see everything." Timothy said looking deep into Lydia's eyes. Timothy was finally beginning to understand the choice the old turtle described to him and the pathway from his vision. Everything was becoming clear to him. His pursuit of vengeance wasn't about justice; it was about his fear. Fear of losing anyone ever again. He would rather lose himself to rage than risk losing someone close to him again. He had seen where that path leads now, and he found himself willing to face his fear in order to take a different path. He had been brave in following a human path, but he felt he could now be brave enough to simply be a mouse again. Sometimes, to be one's true self is the bravest life one can live.

A long enough time had passed in deep contemplation as the two just looked into each other's eyes until it had just begun to become awkward. Timothy, unsure of this new path of being a mouse, thinking to himself what would a mouse say? He wanted to say everything, but the flow of thought was so overwhelming and left him speechless. Lydia looked down to break eye contact, overjoyed with his recovery but unsure about the awkward silence. "I am glad to see you up and about. There were days where we worried if you would pull through."

Toby came running up to them with a rolled up tan colored cloth in his hand. He waddled over to Timothy with a big grin on his face. "We made this for you." Toby said as he placed the rolled cloth in Timothy's hands. "We used some of your human magic."

Timothy unrolled the cloth in his lap. In it was a strange looking small contraption. It was a peanut shell with a metal nail poking through the base of it. It had layers of padding made from fabric patches inside covering the nail head that went through the peanut shell. The shell had holes poked throughout it with string woven through it leading to a laced top with a series of knots. Timothy looked it over, a little confused as to what he was looking at. Lydia looked at him tenderly, "Let me help you try it on." She took the gift from Timothy's lap into her hands and adjusted the laces. She placed the opening of the peanut shell over Timothy's leg stump and shimmied it up tight to his hip. She began tightening the laces around his stump. "It might take some time to get used to it, but I tested it myself, and it's very sturdy." Toby said excitedly, tapping his finger tips together. Timothy didn't quite understand at first, but once it was fitted on, he began to comprehend what they had done for him.

Toby reached out and took Timothy by the hand, lifting him to his foot. "Take it easy but try to put some weight on it." Lydia recommended. Timothy placed the metal tip of his new appendage to the ground and leaned onto it. He gestured to Toby to release his hands, and he shifted his weight to his foot and then moved the peg leg forward again. He did it again and then he looked up at his friends and smiled. He looked down and placed his hand around his new leg and admired its craftsmanship. "How did you all create this?" Timothy inquired.

"It took a few steps. But I'll let you guess what step one was." Toby said with a smirk. "I tied the knots." Lydia said proudly. "You are both truly amazing." Timothy said sincerely. He then stood up tall and took a few more steps. Toby gestured to Timothy to follow him, "You must come and try a blackberry." Timothy panicked as he remembered the precious cargo that was intended to protect Lydia's home, the blackberry bush. "Your cargo, the dried peppers, were you able to salvage them?" Timothy asked concerned.

"No." Lydia answered. "But we found something better." she smirked. Timothy looked at them both puzzled. "We simply inform all the birds who visit this bush that it is now under the protection of the great and magical Timothy Gray." Lydia said braggingly, because it was her idea. "Now, instead of over harvesting our bush, animals come from all around and actually leave gifts. Can you believe that?" She pointed out into the clearing, at a pile of items, food, human debris and even a small book that had been rather weathered and abused with the words Flowers For Algernon, scribed up the spine. "Some are asking for help, others just wanted to show appreciation." Lydia continued. "They call us wizards." Toby said with a laugh. "Yes, even Toby here has developed quite the reputation after single handedly slaying a coyote." Lydia said, almost too dramatically. Timothy looked over at Toby who raised his eyes as if to act ignorant of how such rumors are started. Timothy remembered how few knew the truth about how he defeated the fox and thought maybe it is sometimes best not to pry out the details of such epic tales.

Toby looked up and reached high into the bush to grab a very ripe blackberry and pluck it from its pedicel. He handed it to his friend who continued to hobble along on his new metal leg.

"Oh, speaking of visitors. You have a strange trio here to

see you. The bird said you were friends.." Lydia exclaimed, having just now remembered after being excited to see Timothy finally able to get around and see clearly again.

"A bird? " Timothy asked.

Lydia responded, "Yes, a bird with a goose and a strange old shelled fellow, I believe she said her name was My Lady? Such a strange name for a mocking bird."

Timothy's eyes grew wide as he bit into the blackberry while hearing the news. He turned to Lydia and requested, "Can we fetch my cape?"

The Epic Of Timothy Gray

Chapter Twenty-one
The Saga Continues

Timothy and Toby cleaned the blackberry stains from their
mouths and fetched Timothy's clothes and sword. Timothy
was quickly adapting to hopping around between his one
good foot and his new peg leg. Lydia led them out of the
blackberry hovel and out to a nearby tree where Philis the
mockingbird stood next to a young goose that Timothy
did not recognize. They seemed to be sharing stories and
laughing together. Timothy approached and Philis stopped
speaking when he stepped into her view.

"Well, if it isn't the fearless mouse." Philis perked up. "Philis,
how nice to see you again." Timothy said excitedly. Phillis
turned her head and scrunched her face up to express
dissatisfaction with his greeting. "My lady," He corrected as

he bowed down to her.

"Much better." she perked up. Timothy hobbled on his pegleg. "It is nice to see you made it past the barrier in, mostly, one piece." Phillis commented looking down at his new prosthetic leg. "Yes, I am learning to walk anew, I am afraid it will take some getting used to." Timothy spoke with an optimistic smile.

"I see. There is much new about you my brave mouse friend." Phillis said, looking at Timothy's other side where he had, almost unaware, continued to hold Lydia's hand. He was embarrassed, but he didn't let go. "Yes. Oh, yes. I uh, I am indebted to my new friend, this is Lydia." Timothy stuttered.

"I have had the pleasure of making her acquaintance. My lady." Phillis said as she bowed down before Lydia respectfully. Lydia smiled and covered her mouth out of embarrassment, unsure how to respond.

"Timothy, in my travels I have come across a couple of adventurers who seek an audience with you." The goose had walked up closer to Timothy and was now towering over him. She didn't hesitate to reach down and scoop Timothy into her wings and squeeze him tightly. Timothy wasn't sure what was going on, that is, until he was sat back down to the ground and he looked up into her face. He couldn't quite place the face he was seeing, but it was familiar all the same. "Let me introduce you Timothy, this is Dorathy Gray." Dorathy walked over to Toby and hugged his neck as well.

Toby responded, "Well haven't you grown little Dorothy."

Timothy shook his head in disbelief. Could this be the tiny gosling that they had saved from the clutches of the snake? She had grown nearly four times in size. "Dorothy Gray?" Timothy said, emphasizing the last part of the name into a question.

"My mother named me after the hero that saved my life when I was a mere baby." Dorathy responded. "I also wear this every day to remember you both." She puffed up her chest and buried within her feathery plumage was a necklace made of string, and hanging from that bit of string was a dried snake rattler. As she lifted the rattler up it made a slight noise, "I wear it to remind me to be brave." She shook it a little and it still made that familiar sound of terror that sent shivers down Timothy's spine. "Mother would tell me often of how you two, a mouse and a opossum, selflessly placed their own lives on the line, for me, a little baby gosling." She spoke as a tear came to her eye, "That is the kind of brave goose I wish to be. One who puts others first and is not afraid to stare down the nose of a villainous hunter and say NO MORE!" She gestured with her wing as if she was wielding a sword.

"It is so splendid to see you again Dorothy." Timothy said in shock, "How did you all find us?"

"Oh there are many whispers on the wind about your adventures Timothy" Philis explained, "But the latest stories that we heard informed us to look for the black berry bushes and that came from a very reliable scissor tailed flycatcher who heard it from a group of brown winged cowbirds who said they got the tale right off the back side of the elder of the bison herd."

Timothy and Toby looked at each other with knowing looks and big smiles. This means that Ulysses not only survived crossing the barrier but made it back to his herd.

Timothy tried to step towards Philis wanting to hear more but he hobbled again nearly falling as she caught him.

"I see you misplaced your foot Timothy, quite a shame, but I do like your replacement." Philis joked pointing out Timothy's new prosthetic.

"Thank you, yes, afraid a coyote got it." Timothy explained holding out his new pointed appendage.

"I'm sure you will be dancing on it soon enough." Phillis encouraged. "Jeremiah will be sad to hear you were facing off with coyotes on your own."

"Oh how is ol' Jerebear?" Timothy asked.

"Getting fatter every day. He does ask about you though. I keep him updated with all that I hear in the forest breeze." Phillis said proudly. "Speaking of old friends, I hope you don't mind. I helped a friend of yours navigate here to see you. He said it was urgent that he locate you."

Timothy looked around. All those who he would dare to call friends seemed to be here with him already. He gave a puzzled look.

"He is a rather cryptic and old armadillo. He asked to speak to you alone. He awaits you just past that large boulder over there." Phillis gestured to a large stone just beyond the shade of where they now stood.

"Let us all pick some berries and prepare a meal together, while Timothy speaks with his friend." Lydia injected herself into the conversation. "I'm sure you are all famished from your long journey."

They all departed into the berry bushes leaving Timothy to hop on his new foot, slowly stepping his way out to the boulder. Lydia watched him closely but knew that he would have to practice on his new foot to become accustomed to it. Toby leaned over to Lydia and whispered "I think he will be okay. More than okay really. I am glad Timothy has found a new home."

"You know Toby, you have a home here as well. None of us would be here if it wasn't for your bravery." Lydia said as she reached over and placed a hand on his broad shoulder.

"I don't really burrow down in one place for long, I find it safer to always be moving. It's best for me to not have a home." Toby responded.

"Come and go as you feel, my courageous friend, but know this…" she spoke softly rubbing his shoulder, "you will always have a place to call home. Near or far, you wander as you please but never think that you have not a home. There is no shelter so strong, no hovel so secure, as the one you have when you are with friends." Lydia spoke encouragingly.

"Thank you Lydia." Toby responded as they walked deeper into the blackberry bush surrounded by friends, new and old.

Meanwhile, just over the hedge and behind a large moss-covered boulder sits a mouse with a peg leg, hooded in a crimson cloak with a steel blade strapped to his hip listening intently as an old armadillo spoke boldly and fervently about secrets of the forest and alliances of old. He waved his walking stick energetically as he recounted legends of the mystic ways and the deep magic reserved only for the elect, those chosen by the God of all creation to maintain the sacred balance of nature. After a long-winded explanation of all these things and more, the armadillo turned to Timothy, looking him deep in the eye. "What say you mouse? Will you answer the most sacred call? Will you swear the oath of our ancestors? Will you serve on the council of the forest?"

The Saga Continues

The End

Thank you for taking the time to read my first
novel. Remember, there is no story, no life,
too small or insignificant. We are all worthy of
love and there is always room in any narrative
for redemption. Be the hero in your story and
never let your status determine your influence.
You are capable of great magic, if first you
simply believe it to be possible.